THE OASIS OF HOPE

By

MATTHEW NEWELL

ISBN-13: 978-1539190684
ISBN-10: 1539190684

DEDICATION

To Kathryn, my guiding light.

Thanks to Graham for your brutal honesty and sincere words.

Thanks to Sylvia for believing in me.

CONTENTS

A key, a simple shiny metal key to a home, that holds a soul's earthly wealthy possessions, is considered by some to be the most valuable item that anyone could ever own.

A key, a golden key like the one to a city, is possibly regarded by some to be the greatest gift to ever be received.

Although these keys are symbolic in their own right, they are in fact just plain and simple keys of a material nature.

If you're dead, you have no use for them, you cannot take them with you, they become worthless scraps of metal.

But there is a key, one so precious that it can't be touched or held, like the key to Heaven. That's worth more than life itself.

1

THE GUARDIAN OF THE UNCLAIMED

William Last had returned from the war that still raged on. It had felt like an eternity, but finally he had been summoned back, fresh in his mind to reap his reward for past efforts. His first visit to the sacred place he was heading for was still so memorable.

He was brought here, as a newcomer, by his then great protector in life, his own personal guardian, who had passed down to him the knowledge and deep understanding of the afterlife.

It took Will a long time to adjust but it certainly helped him come to terms and cope with his own mortality in those early days upon arrival at this the astral plane to which he seemed eternally tied and on which the Oasis of Hope once flourished before everything went to hell!

As Will hiked across the uneven and crumbling hillside path he walked on, he reflected back to his old mentor. His mentor back then, too, was a guardian of an unclaimed soul and had served the position well for almost thirty years until it was time to collect his charge, Will, from Earth.

Now his mentor had earned his wings and had literally taken flight. Will wished for nothing more than to earn his too and be reunited with his old mentor in paradise.

Looking up to the crest of the hill, Will gazed upon which path he should take. He could take the weathered, loose stone-chipped path that snaked off to the west, or he could cut north and climb the treacherous jagged rocks and boulder-strewn path ahead.

Time was of the essence, though, and Will felt although the path to the north was more dangerous, it was also the quickest. Being exposed too long out in plain sight could attract soul stealers and Will knew that was not an option he wanted to take. He was too weary and battle scarred to put up much of a fight.

He took one last look back to the valley below and saw dark fog rolling in from the south wilds, and decided there and then to make a break for the north route. Who knows what the fog could be hiding!

Will marched near the brow of the hill looking for a foothold in the jagged rocks and boulders to pull himself up and over. He gazed out to the sky hanging listless and still. The sky burnt orange and a darkness radiated from within, signalling hard times ahead.

Will stumbled on loose chippings and fell down upon his left knee, cursing himself for not watching where he was going. He cast his eyes down to the tattered hem of his overcoat and realised it was still smouldering with rank smoke from his near miss earlier.

He picked himself up and continued on his now

3

progressively steeper ascent. A path had opened up to him, but required he climb up onto the nearest rock by using a nearby boulder to leap from. From there it would be a matter of a few leaps of faith to the adjoining rocks and he would be home free.

The wind whistled down through the craggy outcrop and Will steeled himself for the task ahead. His last act of defiance to make it to the Oasis to visit Thalamus.

He hoped that by conversing with Thalamus, at the Oasis, that all his past efforts would grant him his wings. But Will truly knew that it wasn't assured and that his summoning could be for something else entirely. He just hoped for a second chance to right his wrongs.

Will pulled his lapels up around his face and made his final steps. He hauled himself onto the nearby boulder and readied himself for the jump to the rock. He lunged, and as he did so the wind caught him and nearly threw him off balance. His fingertips barely made contact with the ledge. He reached down with his foot and found a niche and pushed off to finally reach the top of the rock. With a hop here and a skip there and a final jump to the peak, he had cleared the obstacles in his way.

The breath-taking view of the valley on the other side spread out before him and the orange glow from the sinking sun hit the contours of the land below, picking out the colour of a path made entirely of wild flowers that he must take deep down at its lowermost point. Steadily behind it, the dark clouds came.

A mix of autumn snowflake, ground elder,

pyramidal orchid, and prickly poppy, amongst others, all intermingled and stretched off into the distance like the colours of a rainbow paving the way before him. The end of the path was overshadowed by a large expanse of forest that it crept into, and Will could just make out the remnants of an ancient crumbling wall, just within its borders. It brought great hope to Will and made him smile, for he knew his journey was coming to an end. He would make it before his tainting took hold.

He adjusted himself and descended towards the vale and on towards the path, leaving his troubles behind him back over the hill. He knew the path could only be tread by the pure and that no evil could follow him upon reaching it. The path's end to the secret resting place of the Oasis.

*

The path of flowers became more sparse as he ventured into the dark forest with barely any light left from the diminishing sun on the horizon. As the last light faded through the thick canopies, the path ended before the ancient wall border.

Will clambered over and found himself in a clearing. Two of eight giant, white, marbled stone pillars, well-spaced to allow a party of five through side by side, loomed before him. Both of the pillars had crumbled midway and the tops were abandoned by their side. Six more pillars, still erect, opened up in a horseshoe formation past the crumbled pillars and vines were growing over them all, connecting them to one another. Lily of the valley entwined around them.

Sensing he was near, Will slowed his pace. The

hairs on the back of his neck tingled as the dread of some malevolent foreboding took hold of him. The quiet of his surroundings made him feel uneasy. Not a bird or cricket could be heard.

Will turned to look back up the path. Seeing there was no presence behind him, but not taking any risks, he quickened his pace and made a dash for the opening.

As he passed between the two marbled pillars that straddled the path's nearing end, Will gazed all around. He took in the vista of the other six pillars stretched out before him. They stretched around a moat of a bubbling, tainted green stream, lapping at the edges, acting like sentries. At the centre stood an overgrown island, densely populated with wild thorn bushes and wild fauna. At its middle, a small granite rock, on which sat a two-handled metal chalice, undisturbed by time.

When Will last visited the scene was much different. The lake was a shimmering blue and the island was a lush green grass meadow, abundant with wild sunflowers and insects gathering pollen. Evil had no time to take hold back then.

Will hoped that the healing properties of the lake were not tainted and that some regenerating traces remained, as he was in desperate need of recharging. Even in death, regeneration was needed to sustain life even though food was not.

Will walked sombrely to the edge of the moat and knelt down; he could hardly make out his reflection in the clockwise-flowing lake. *Which is just as well*, Will thought.

The last reflection Will had come to see of himself

was of a youthful man in his mid-thirties, slim built with sharp features and a full lock of jet black hair.

Time had surely not been kind since, with the constant battles taking place all around him, in which he had been heavily involved. All of Will's pains ebbed back again as his adrenaline from the journey subsided.

Will looked at the palm of his left hand and picked away at a deep charred gorge that cut across it vertically. He remembered the whip that had flailed his way and that his quick sense of grabbing the end with his hand had prevented a greater target being made. The whip was yanked back but the sharp steel tip that was attached to the end had sliced through his palm, causing the deep scar. Will pushed his hand into the lake and prayed the wound would heal.

Sure enough, the very essence of the water seemed to soak into the cut, coating it with a pale green residue, and Will could feel the hurt being erased from existence.

Will pulled his hand out and studied it. Now just a white faded scar was left and Will flexed his hand to be sure that the water had done its healing.

Happy that the Oasis was not compromised and seriously needing to be healed all over, Will stood up, looked across to the island that was three hundred yards or so away, and dived in. The instant rush of well-being and rejuvenation seeped into his every pore.

As he swam in the cool depths he felt himself being refreshed and revitalised after the arduous journey he had been on. The water on his lips, however, tasted like battery acid. The taint of evil was trying to contaminate the pureness of the lake. But at the same time it was all in a state of flux, and stalemate was being met by opposing forces.

Eventually he came to the bank of the island and feeling less weary and a little stronger, he pulled himself up onto the flat.

He made his way over to the hard black granite, avoiding the brambles as he did. He hesitated for a bit and then swiftly reached out and plucked the silver steel chalice from its resting place.

'Well Thalamus, I've finally made it,' Will shouted triumphantly, knowing he would be heard.

He knew this ritual only too well, so was not surprised that with a creak and a groan the granite began to descend into the depths of the island.

Will knew that the next part of the ritual would be less joyous, seeing as how he still had the taste of the lake on his lips. The thought of what would come next reviled him.

The lake's flow began to take up momentum as it circled the island, moving faster and faster; the noise became more deafening as it did so.

Suddenly it rose above the island but still circling it, whilst not spilling over onto the island or the land across the far bank. It formed an impenetrable, high, continuous, flowing wall.

It levelled out with the tops of the still-intact pillars and created a liquid wall that shut off the island on all sides.

Will smiled and held the chalice with both hands.

He studied an engraving of a pair of wings on its face and rubbed his thumb in the hollowed-out shape. He knew that a key matching the engraving slotted into it, but that he did not possess it. He was also aware of its purpose and it gave him hope. He wished the agenda for today would resolve his conflict, as he who holds the winged key would be granted their wings. Will prayed that it would be his time to receive them and then he could leave all this behind forever.

Will took the chalice and strode over to the fast-flowing high wall of cloudy green water and plunged the chalice in.

Within moments the chalice was overflowing with the dark, tainted, green water, that had built up a residue of froth around the rim of the cup.

Removing the full cup, Will placed the rim to his mouth. He gulped at the thought of drinking the tainted water and tipped it into his mouth. As the water slid down his throat and the froth transferred to his lips, Will doubled over with the feeling of nausea, as the acidic taste slid down his throat. He dropped the chalice and fell to his knees before retching at the burning taste.

He barely had time to remove the froth from his mouth, when the lake began to recoil in reverse and suddenly Will was thrust up into the air by an unseen force, and slowly he was spun around.

He gazed down to the island below and then back to the topmost of the water wall, which was at eye height as he tried to steady his gaze.

It was then, over the sound of the roaring water, that the whispering voices of Thalamus came to him from everywhere at once and resonated through his very being.

2

POSTCARDS FOR THE HODOPHOBIC

The travel agents building stood proudly, tucked away within a long a string of other businesses, its high glass windows advertising cheap holiday deals to various destinations around Europe and beyond.

The high street was awash with people going about their daily lives, perusing the shop windows and occasionally going in to do their shopping. The travel agency had a few customers cast their looks into the window to see if they could afford their dream holiday, and chattered amongst themselves of where they would most like to visit.

One such couple were just exiting the travel agents and were still in conversation about the holiday that they had just come back from. As the door swung shut behind Mr and Mrs Dumont's exit, Stan waved them off with a cheery smile. He studied the postcard that they had given him only a short while ago. *If only I could visit places like this,* he thought.

Stanley Palmer had worked in the travel sector for a little over twenty years. He had never been on holiday once in his life, but he pertained to know everything about each country and its origin within.

He would take the new holiday brochures home whenever a new one came out and pore over the glossy pictures. He would research all the villas he saw and go onto the web to find them and take a virtual tour, imagining that he was actually there and the sights and sounds that would greet him.

He was a top salesman who was adored by his customers for the knowledge he shared about their holiday choices. Even to the point they would bring back postcards for him, to be pinned up on his wall.

Stan would often share with his customers his plight of having a phobia that had prevented him from leaving the country, and for them to come back to him with their holiday antics.

He turned his latest postcard over in his hand, it read: *"To Stan, thanks for the great recommendation, we look forward to seeing you next year."* He flipped the card back round and gazed into the image, pretending he could step into its frame and be swallowed up by the grand vista that lay before him.

Snapping him out of his deep thought, a female voice piped up behind him. 'See you got another one for your wall then, Stan?'

'What? Sorry. Yeah, yeah I have. Number...' He hesitated. 'Number sixty-six I think... for my collection of postcards. Here, take a look.'

Stan swivelled round and offered the postcard across to the person behind him.

Natasha received the card and looked at the glossy

print. 'Greetings from Hell's Kitchen,' she said. 'Nice. Different from the usual ones you get, shame you will never get over your phobia to visit somewhere like Manhattan, hey?'

Swinging the chair back round to his desk to avoid embarrassment, Stan said regrettably, 'No, probably not. I've tried therapy but never followed it through. I clammed up trying to talk about my past. Figured some things are best left alone. I can make do without it.'

'You're fooling yourself, Stan. Think of all the holidays you've missed out on with your wife and kids. That's got to be hard, right?' Natasha didn't wait for a response. 'So this phobia of yours that stops you travelling anywhere. What's it called again?'

Stan looked up from his desk. 'Hodophobia. Look, I don't want to sound rude, but you're not going to get out of me how I came to have it, okay?'

'Sure Stan, whatever you say. I just think it's a shame is all.' Natasha placed a hand on his shoulder for reassurance and slid the postcard across his desk. 'At least our customers are satisfied, going by the postcards you're collecting and all... You know, you'll probably die in this village without ever seeing the rest of the world,' she said, pointing at the plethora of postcards. 'You've never lived until you've been abroad,' she added wistfully. With that, Natasha turned away and made her way back to her desk.

Stan looked at the postcard depicting a row of quaint little shops all of different colours, nestled together, lining a street, and noted comparisons between there and his town. He picked it up along with a pin and stuck it to his cork board that hung adjacent his desk.

Just then, Stan's work phone rang. He picked it up, flustered. 'He... hello, Tower Travel Agents. Stan speaking. How may I help?'

'Stan it's me, Petra. Sorry to ring you at work but I wanted to remind you that I'm collecting you by car today. I'll be there at five, is that okay?'

The realisation of what today meant and the ramifications came flooding back to him all at once.

He felt his heart beginning to race and his hand that held the phone began to shake. He looked around to make sure no one was watching.

The past came back to him. The bus. The approaching vehicle. The ravine and the river. Stan felt the perspiration building on the back of his neck. He wasn't sure but he could feel his chest tighten. Or was it cramp? He couldn't be sure.

'Stan? Hello? Are you still there?' Petra said.

Finally he answered through a dry mouth, 'Yeah, sorry darling. Look, I thought we discussed this earlier this morning? I'm just not sure I'm ready for a lift in the car just yet.'

Silence followed.

Stan looked gloomily around and reached down to his desk drawer and pulled out a small bottle of anti-anxiety pills. He unscrewed the lid, tipped two pills into his free hand, re-screwed the lid shut and popped it back into the drawer, nudging it shut.

'Stan, you're worrying me. Talk to me please?' Petra said solemnly.

'Sorry, I'm listening,' Stan replied. He threw the pills into his mouth and reached across his desk, picking up a half-drunk bottle of water.

'This is nonsense,' she added. 'It's twenty minutes back by car or an hour with you walking. The girls are at home waiting for you and we have a special surprise for your birthday today. You're not going to keep us all waiting now, are you Stan Palmer?' she added.

Stan pressed the bottle of water to his lips and swallowed the pills down with force.

You're being ridiculous. Get a grip, Stan. It will be okay. It's just a short trip and nothing will go wrong, he thought.

Stan felt himself beginning to relax.

'Okay,' he said reluctantly, 'but I warn you – if I start freaking out then I want you stop and let me out. Alright?'

'Yeah sure, that's fine. just promise me you won't lose it though, cause the girls and me really want you to have a memorable day today. After all, you're only forty once!'

'Gee, thanks for reminding me. Just cause you've got a couple more years to reach it, you don't have to rub it in,' Stan said, feeling a little better.

Petra laughed. 'That's more like it. A sense of humour, that will see you home in no time. Anyway, I gotta go. I'll see you in a bit. Love you!'

'Love you too,' Stan replied. With that the line went dead. Stan gave a big sigh of relief; the impending sense of doom had passed, although he knew that the real test would be getting into the car later.

Natasha walked past Stan's desk with a cup of coffee in her hand.

'Your wife's lucky to have you. I can't believe she would try and force you into something you didn't want to do though,' she said, passing Stan the coffee.

'Err, thanks. She means well.'

'I'm sure she does. I mean look at you. You're quite the catch with your rugged good looks and your heart-melting smile. If I was a few years younger I'd make a play for you myself,' Natasha said soothingly.

'We wouldn't be a good match. I prefer brunettes to blondes!' Stan said jokingly, feeling a little awkward. 'Anyway, you're not much older than me. I'm sure there's someone still out there looking for someone like you,' he added, trying to change the conversation. 'I was lucky finding my soulmate at twenty-one. Your soulmate may just be round the corner, don't you think?'

Natasha flicked her hair and turned on the spot.

'Maybe, Stan. Maybe...' She added, 'Enjoy your coffee.' With that, she headed off out to the back of the office.

Stan checked his watch. It read 4.30PM.

Today will be the death of me, Stan thought. He looked up to his growing collection of postcards on the wall.

'Sixty-six postcards, and number sixty-six is of Hell's Kitchen. What are the odds?' he said aloud. He hoped it wasn't a bad omen.

3

DE'ATH CUMMINGS' FUNERAL

The black hearse with its procession of traffic drove steadily along. The cars behind were increasing with every junction that the hearse passed.

The dying sun shone off the highly polished black exterior, forcing its two front passengers to lower their visors to avoid the glare bouncing off the hood into their eyes.

The hearse driver tapped the digital speedometer.

'It's on the blink again, Reg,' he said. He knew he had to tell the old funeral director every little detail or risk reprisal.

'Overdue a service,' Reg said matter-of-factly. 'What's it say?'

'Park brake fault. Will that be a problem with the church we're going to, sitting on a hill and all?' he replied.

Reg thought for a minute then said, 'No, don't worry. It's electrical, not mechanical. It showed me the same message the other day when I went to fill it up.'

'OK, you're the boss. I'll look to book it in when we've a quiet day then.'

One of the pall bearers in the back spoke. 'I don't wish to add to any hiccups, but it's been raining this morning and the ground is still wet. We ought to take care when we move the coffin, just in case.' He said it more for his own concern than anyone else, as he knew how precarious it could be carrying a coffin on your shoulder, especially underfoot.

'You've carried before, Paul. You'll be fine,' Reg said.

The hearse pulled onto the motorway and the traffic behind started to accelerate to get past in the fast lane.

'It's not me I'm worried about. It's poor old De'Ath, bless him!' he exclaimed more as a statement.

De'Ath Cummings didn't hear the comment. He just rode comfortably along without a care in the world.

Life for De'Ath had been trivial. In his younger years he had grafted hard in the property market, with his inheritance money, and had bought many houses to renovate and then leased them out. On making his money, he had divorced his wife and had a fling with a young woman half his age. He realised it was a mistake too late and his wife fleeced him for half his wealth, and the young woman had left him penniless from what he had left over and ran off with it.

He knew that he had been a foolish man, but he was now past caring.

Paul cut the silence. 'So where's the rest of the pall

bearers then, Reg? Cause this guy in the coffin weighs a ton. He's a big fella!' he asked.

'Meeting us at the church. Hopefully they've set up the music and have dropped off the order of service booklets.'

'It's an awfully late one today though, don't you think Reg? I've never attended a funeral at this late hour before,' the hearse driver said.

'No, me neither, but the customer in the back there has an awful lot of friends and family coming from all over, so I guess it was arranged for that time so everyone could turn out to pay their respects.' He then added, 'If all goes well, then you will still make it home for six, depending on rush hour of course.'

'Traffic's tight. Bumper to bumper already. I don't suppose we are helping much,' the hearse driver noted, looking into his wing mirror at the traffic building up behind again.

Reg then turned to the driver. 'That reminds me, I forgot to ask. You did make sure the coffin was locked tight in the back there?' Reg pointed over his shoulder to the coffin rubber wheel guides.

'Yup,' came the reply.

'...As close to the coffin at both adjacent ends? And the head stopper screwed up tight to stop it shifting forwards and backwards?' he said without a breath.

'Yup,' replied the hearse driver.

'You sure?'

'U-huh,' he replied, but he knew deep down that he had overlooked checking both.

'Cool. I noticed the head spray of flowers looks good on top of the lid. Not sure about the named wreath though, at the head of the coffin,' Reg mused.

'Oh, I don't know. I think you can see that coming.' Paul laughed.

'Less of the joking, Paul. This is not the place for that.'

'Sorry,' came the reply.

The rest of the journey was had in relative silence.

For De'Ath, the peace and silence was all he ever wanted.

As the coffin he lay in rocked backwards and forwards over the rollers it sat upon, and his named flower wreath was slowly nudged toward the hearse rear window with each rocking motion, his corpse seemed finally at peace.

The white-haired hearse driver smiled at the coffin in the rear-view mirror and wondered what next would lie before De'Ath, as his true journey had really only just begun.

Death is only the beginning. The true test lies in the afterlife, he pondered.

The hearse driver didn't know why he thought this, but somewhere deep down inside, he felt a greater presence was playing its part and that gave him some measure of small comfort that all would turn out good.

He also couldn't put his finger on it, but he sensed something extraordinary was going to happen today, and his own contribution to it would be a big deciding factor in the outcome.

4

MALA SORT RIVER

The whispers circled round and round Will's levitated body, growing more fervent as each word from Thalamus hit him like exploding fireworks.

'William, welcome back. I pray your journey was uninterrupted.' The whispers were made up of a mixture of female and male voices.

'Yes, I was not followed!' Will shouted against the deafening wind and the sound of the lake, which thundered in every direction.

'Straight to business then. We haven't much time,' came the whispering again, in a calm steady stream within the chaotic vortex around it.

Droplets from the lake's spray, combined with the circling wind, pelted Will all at once from all around.

'Am I to leave and go claim the unclaimed?' Will bellowed.

'You shall, but first I need to share information that you will need in order to complete your task,' Thalamus answered.

'I understand. You have my full cooperation,' Will

exclaimed whilst unintentionally sucking in the bitter taste of the lake that splattered his face.

'As you are most certainly aware, we are losing the fight. I have, however, recently learned that there is a reason we do not succeed. One that even I did not see coming. The evil that taints all it touches has found a new way to do us harm. It has been dormant too long. I fear it knows what's coming.'

'What harm is it you speak of?' Will questioned after wiping the taste from his lips with thumb and forefinger.

'Good and pure unclaimed souls that are brought here by their Guardians, are being targeted and taken to the Tower to have their very essence converted to evil and malice before the split of the river has even decided their fate. As for their Guardians, they just vanish from existence.' The whispers took on a new tone and Thalamus sounded hollow and defeated.

'I will find out how and why this is happening then,' Will said glumly, and added, 'I will make sure that the lost soul I will take has a chance too.'

'No, this is not my intention. I know the evil has saved the life of this lost soul of yours that you are referring to, many years ago, and even though that soul is pure, I have put into motion an event that will force him to sin. In turn, this will seal his fate and turn him back to us.'

'Why would you do this?' Will sounded puzzled. 'I don't understand. This is going to jeopardise my chances of getting my wings.' He felt himself getting angry. How dare he be robbed of his one and only chance to achieve his only desire.

Thalamus sensed Will's anger and brought the circling lake that rose high to reach over the island to gel, forming an impenetrable dome of water.

The space around Will darkened as the light was blocked out and static began to build all around him.

As if at once, lightning shot out from all around.

Will's thoughts were that if he were an outsider looking in right now, this event would resemble that of an electric plasma ball with Will himself at the centre.

The excruciating electrified pulses that hit Will sent him plummeting to the ground, his wet clothes crackling and beginning to smoulder. Then as if on cue, the lightning ceased.

Will lay still and motionless, smoke rising off his clothes.

The wind picked up again and as it did it pulled Will straight back up into the air. Smoke began to exhume from him in a whirl as he was slowly spun again.

Thalamus' voice raged, *'You and your lost soul will be sacrificed for the greater good and that should be enough for you, Will.'*

Will realised his error and knew not to question anymore, but to accept his faith. 'OK, I will do as you request,' he said, defeated. But a dark thought occurred to him. A realisation that there was more than one way to get his wings.

'You will save this lost soul that you have been the Guardian of, and avoid damning his fate until I send word. I have a proposition for him before I send him to his fate. I don't want the evil that bleeds across our astral plane to know that we are onto it. This is our chance to gain a foothold into the war we face.' Thalamus' voice had trailed off to

whispers again.

Will gingerly asked a question. 'So if the evil steals enough souls to convert, it in turn will diminish our numbers. It will break the confines of the tower, sweep the plane, and overthrow us all. Am I correct in saying this?'

'Yes,' came the whisper, *'but we will not let this happen. Stan will see to it that we succeed and if he fails then his second chance at life will be taken away and his soul will be forever lost, and also that of his fellow man.'*

'Forgive me for asking more questions, but how will Stan achieve this and what will become of me?' Will said quizzically, with the smoke wafting around him from his charred and tattered clothes. His anger brewed inside.

'All in good time,' came the reply. *'Now it is time for you to depart. Good luck.'* The whispers began to fade.

With that, Will looked down to his feet. Below him the island started to peel away into a black precipice.

With a sudden boom, Will was released from his levitated grip and like a bullet fired down the barrel of a gun, he shot down into the dark black void of nothingness, chasing the descending island that was vanishing before his sight. Before he could get his bearings, the sound of the lake gushing overhead gave way and as Will cast his gaze up, it too came crashing down upon him, chasing him into the expanse.

*

As Will resurfaced, he spat out a lungful of water and realised he had descended to earth and found himself in the middle of a river surrounded by a shoal of dead fish floating around him, of various colours and species.

Will batted some fish that were in his way to make a clear path, and swam for shore.

He pulled himself out onto the lush green bank. Sitting on the edge of the bank with his feet still dangling in the water, Will collected himself and looked out across the river, past the dead fish to the far bank.

He noticed a sign nestled within the bushes. It was a wooden plaque and the lettering on it was flaking and weathered. It read:

MALA SORT RIVER

NO SWIMMING

NO FISHING

Will's smile widened. It wasn't every day he had a chance to come back to visit. *Shame no one can see me, but at least I can witness the final moments of Stan's life,* he thought, *and it's going to happen right here. For you, Stan, the end is coming, but with it a chance to do some good.*

Gazing back behind him, Will noticed the steep incline of the riverbank leading up to a steel crash barrier that separated the road from this descent down to the river.

Beyond the road was an interconnecting road spurring off to form a T-junction where the road then ran up a hill. A church sat magnificently at its top to the left.

Will climbed the ascent and hopped over the crash barrier, to take in a better view of his surroundings.

Past the church was where Will knew the town started, and in it was the premises that Stanley Palmer worked.

Will perched himself on the crash barrier and gazed around. Life was teeming everywhere, the birds in the trees singing, cars driving back and forth, people walking their dogs. It was almost too overwhelming for him to be this close to a previous way of life all over again.

Everything looks perfect, all that I can do now is wait, Will thought.

For Will, this meant waiting for Stan and himself to be reunited once more, but at least now to talk to each other at last, instead of Will just being Stan's reasoning and logic in his life's decision making behind the scenes.

5

COME HELL OR HIGH WATER

Petra swiped her mobile phone to end her call and slung it casually onto the passenger seat. She turned the key in the ignition, looked in the rear-view to check her makeup still looked good and that her short, bobbed, brunette hair was not out of place against her elongated features.

She then gave a further glance to make sure nothing was coming behind her, indicated, and pulled out onto the open road.

She loved her little car. It gave her an enormous sense of joy being able to go where she wanted, when she wanted.

The car had been a tenth anniversary present from Stan last year. She had hoped that when he had got it for her, that it was his way of finally getting over his phobia and that he was ready to lay his demons to rest.

But it had a reverse effect. He had slowly, over time, come to worry that she would have an accident or something bad was going to happen in it. He constantly told her to be careful whenever she was just popping out in it.

Petra came to realise that Stan would never get over his phobia and truly feel what it was like to have the freedom to travel around. As a neurosurgeon she knew only too well the effects the brain could produce.

As she turned off the main road and onto the slip road which connected to the motorway, she glanced into the rear-view at Stan's present on the back seat as she sidled into the slow lane.

The present was rectangular in shape, a foot long, and had been wrapped carefully in blue glitter effect wrapping paper. Holes had been pierced into one end in a grid-like pattern and a handle was poking out of the top, that had not been wrapped over.

The present slid across the back seat; a thud accompanied it followed by a pitiful scratching noise within. 'Damn, sorry little guy. I almost forgot you were in there,' Petra said aloud. 'Tell you what, let's have some music, shall we?'

The sound from the confines of the present came back as a scrabbling noise followed by a thump.

Petra flicked on the radio. A song called "Come Hell or High Water" blasted out over the airwaves. Petra recognised it as a poor remix of a classic song that most music these days had become. She believed that there wasn't much originality left in the world anymore. She grimaced as she flicked the dial down a few notches.

A little further along and she came to a crawl. Both lanes had converged into one. She lowered her window and stuck her head out to get a better look at the road ahead.

She noticed that beyond the eight or so cars in front of her there was a jet black hearse leading the way.

Oh great, now I'm going to be late to pick up Stan, she thought. She pulled her head in and checked her on-board clock. It showed the time – 5.10.

For ten minutes they crawled along. Petra began to tap the steering wheel with her fingertips. Patience was not her best virtue.

Eventually seven cars had turned off at the various junctions they passed, leaving her, only one car, and the hearse in front.

Petra was getting closer to town but also she was becoming more irritable. She noticed to her right that they were now following alongside the Mala Sort River.

It was then that she decided to overtake. She guessed that the hearse would be taking the same route as her. It would be going to the church that she would need to pass to head into town.

A car travelling in the opposite direction seemed far enough away. Petra chanced it and accelerated, pulling out.

As she drew level with the hearse, she read the name made of flowers at the head and it dawned on her whose funeral it was. She remembered Stan talking about De'Ath, whose name the flowers spelled out, and that he had been a good customer.

She realised almost too late that it would be too tight and cut across the path of the hearse, narrowly avoiding the car coming the other way. The driver of the car slammed his horn in anger; Petra's heart was in her mouth. She mouthed 'sorry' at the driver and in turn almost shot past the exit she needed.

Turning off left, she drove up the hill, leaving the Mala Sort River and the hearse in her rear-view mirror.

She passed the church, with the vicar standing outside, waiting with what looked like three pall bearers, one of whom was placing traffic cones down, that she presumed would stop anyone from parking there, when it was reserved for the hearse only.

It was then she saw Stan walking toward her. *Handsome as ever,* she thought. Just under six feet tall, suited and booted with his top button undone on his white shirt. His silk silver tie hung loose around his neck. Petra pulled over and waited for him to get in.

Pulling off a three-point manoeuvre and with Stan safely on board, they continued on their way. Back to their quiet village on the outskirts of town.

*

As Will waited at the bottom of the hill, he noticed a bench nearby facing back up to the hill. On approaching it, he saw it had an engraved plaque screwed into the middle of the back rest. The inscription read:

IN MEMORY OF THOSE
WE LOST TRAGICALLY
IN 1982. MAY THEY BE
FOREVER AT PEACE

Will gazed upon it with saddened eyes and sat down upon it. *So this was where it all started for you, Stan, and this is where it will end,* he thought.

He looked back up the hill with dismay and caught sight of a hearse turning in to take its final drive, to stop at the church at the hilltop.

*

As Petra and Stan drove back down the hill, they passed the hearse coming up. Neither noticed, though, as they were too involved in a heated argument.

Stan was trembling. 'Look, I told you this was a bad idea. We've been over this before, so just let me out and I will walk the rest of the way. OK?' he stammered.

'You've come this far, Stan, and I know you've taken your pills, so what's the problem? Just close your eyes and chill. We will be home before you know it,' Petra retorted as she slowed down for the junction.

Stan rubbed his sweaty palms on his lap and gripped hard onto his knees. 'I'm sorry, but I can't do this. Look up ahead, see that?' He pointed his finger to the river.

'Yeah. So what? It was a long time ago. You should be over that by now. If you had got counselling back when we first met, then you wouldn't even give it a second thought,' Petra said flippantly.

Stan felt the confines of the car closing in. 'I feel sick, let me out. Let me out now!' Stan brought his fist down on the dashboard in a rage.

'God damn it, Stan! Are you really going to ruin this for all of us? Are you?' Petra screamed back at him.

Stan had already pushed open the door and was fighting to get his seatbelt off.

Petra pulled the car over into the hard shoulder and Stan, free from his binds, bolted out and ran to the barrier, panting, and loosened his tie further to gasp for air.

Petra turned off the engine and opened the door, making her way over to Stan.

Raising his hand to stop her approaching, he said, 'Just leave me, I'll be fine.'

'The hell you will, Stan! You could have got us both killed with that crazy shit!'

Stan felt himself getting angrier. 'If you'd have let me just walk home, I would have taken the shortcut through the housing estate as I always do, then I wouldn't be standing here now, back where it all started.'

Petra started to approach him again. 'Alright, I'm sorry, just calm down. Take another pill and we can set off again. Maybe you hadn't taken enough doses?' she said, trying to defuse the situation.

Stan tried to speak, but his breath was laboured and his chest began to tighten again. He tried to focus, but the world was spinning around him.

He vaulted the barrier and with no sense of direction, started to walk down the bank to the river's edge, in a daze.

Petra had gone back to the car and retrieved a packet of cigarettes from the glove compartment. She flipped the lid and prised one out, fumbled for her lighter in her cardigan pocket and continued to light the cigarette using the car as a shield from the wind that was blowing up from the embankment.

As she inhaled the smoke to calm herself down, she remembered the present on the back seat. She reached over and retrieved it. The creature inside fell backwards and then slid forward as she swung the carrier back to the front of the car. 'Sorry kitty, but I need you right now to calm my husband down and stop him drowning in self-pity,' she said in between inhaling the smoke.

By the time Petra had caught Stan up he was on his knees, sobbing at the water's edge. 'Here Stan, take this. It will cheer you up,' she tried to say reassuringly. She offered him his present and discarded the cigarette.

Stan looked up with watery eyes and snatched the present from her grasp. 'I told you, I will make my own way back. No peace gesture is going to make any difference!' he yelled. He threw the present into the river.

Petra cried out, 'Oh my god! No, Stan, what have you done?'

But it was too late, the perforated holes in the carrier had already let in water and it was sinking fast, sealing the kitten within to a watery grave. Only the handle could be seen as it drifted off down the river, buffeting off some dead fish that floated at the surface.

Petra ran, howling and sobbing, back up the incline.

'What? What have I done, Petra?' Stan shouted after her. 'I don't understand,' he wailed as he looked to the handle that sank out of sight.

He pulled himself up and made for the incline just as Petra had pulled herself over the barrier.

*

The hearse pulled up outside the church and the occupants all got out.

'Wait there a minute, lads, I'm just going to go and make sure they're ready for us,' Reg said as he strode over to the vicar and the waiting pall bearers.

The hearse driver looked in through the window to the driver's side and cursed. 'I forgot to turn the engine off, Paul. I'll meet you in a minute.'

Paul acknowledged and began to make his way round past the front of the hearse.

But just as the hearse driver went to grab the handle, the hearse began to roll backwards. The park brake fault warning message flashed lazily in his mind's eye.

All hell broke loose!

The hearse driver yelled for help. All the pall bearers came running. Reg turned in horror too late and realised what was happening.

The hearse picked up momentum as it started its decline downhill. A car coming the opposite way swerved to avoid it and careered across the road, coming to a stop inches from a lamppost. Reg dived for the front of the hearse to grab the bumper, but his hands came away from the highly polished paintwork. The hearse driver slipped and fell. Paul, who had been crossing its path only moments before, had dived out of its way. The three remaining pall bearers looked on in shock and the vicar grabbed his bible tight to his chest and made a silent prayer to God.

The hearse kept a straight line as it passed from view, becoming a black speck on the horizon.

*

Stan barely made it the top of the incline when he heard Petra scream out to him, 'Stan, look out!'

But Stan knew it was too late. Everything then happened as if in slow motion.

The hearse hit the barrier at breakneck speed, coming to an abrupt stop. The impact buckled the boot, the glass shattered into a thousand pieces. The coffin dislodged from the rollers and took flight and left through where the glass once was.

The last thing Stan saw was De'Ath's flowers attached to the head of the coffin heading straight for him, but his mind interpreted it as just simply DEATH, followed by a very heavy oak veneer coffin laden with a very large gentleman inside. The coffin found its mark.

*

Will rose from the bench and made his way over to the scene. He approached the woman who was frantically trying with all her might to prise the coffin off her husband buried beneath it. 'You may see him again soon,' he said. And to Stan, 'You and I have business, this has been a long time coming.'

With that, Will disappeared just as the sun dipped down out of sight on the horizon.

6

THE ROAD LESS TRAVELLED

Stan didn't mind the ride to school, but every so often whilst he was reading his comic, *THE INCREDIBLE ADVENTURES OF THE HUMAN COFFIN FLY #3*, bile formed in the back of his throat and the nausea took hold. It wasn't the first time it had happened.

His mum had tried to remedy his travel sickness with a motion sickness wristband that worked by applying pressure on the Nei Kuan acupressure point, or so she said.

If truth be told, it was hit and miss. Although a young six-year-old, Stan was sure the comic reading wasn't helping matters.

The condensation trickled down the window, built up from the excited talking children who sat with him in the minibus. Five of them in total, not including the driver.

It was an overcast, gloomy, dark morning and already the rain had begun to fall in light droplets as they took their usual route to school.

Driving through an underpass, the road became

very narrow and occasionally the bus would have to pull off hard to the verge to allow the oncoming traffic to get past. Its wheels would on occasion get stuck in ruts and the driver would have to floor it to get out, kicking up loose gravel and mud, covering the side of the vehicle.

The country road they travelled on would become quite bumpy as the bus would rattle along. It would run rather close to the Mala Sort River, named because of the many lives it had claimed over the years. The name was derived from the Catalan word meaning "unlucky". Stan liked to read.

As the minibus worked its way further along the narrow road, it rose higher and away from the river.

Eventually the road wound back round to the edge of the river so that they were almost back upon it, looking down into a ravine with the fast-flowing river below. Stan looked across to the left window and could just make the outline of it. Deep, dark, and unwelcoming.

The driver turned on the headlights just as the rain began to fall harder and then flicked the wipers to their highest setting, the *woosh, woosh* of the wipers intensifying as they struggled to bat the rain from the front window. Visibility gradually became worse. The battering of water hitting the roof echoed around the bus, forcing Stan to fold up and stash his comic in the pocket attached to the rear of the seat in front of him.

The chattering became hushed muffles as the bus slipped and slid on the windy road.

As if out of nowhere a set of headlights rounded the corner, forcing the bus driver to act. He hit the brakes but the bus continued sliding. It hit the oncoming vehicle with its rear end; the seatbelts holding in Stan and the other children tightened as the impact swung the rear of it over the edge.

Stan felt hopeless. The children were screaming. The bus didn't teeter for long. The driver tried to accelerate but there was not enough traction on the front wheels and the rear wheels spun lifelessly over the ravine.

The front of the bus rose into the air and the children were slammed backwards into their seats, as the bus began its rear descent down the ravine and into the cold, dark, waiting river below.

*

As the past flashed through Stan's mind, his circumstance no worse then than it was now, his thoughts drifted back to that night. The bus ended up on its side in the river. The water came pouring in though the smashed windows. Stan, having blacked out on impact, woke and struggled against his seatbelt as the water rose above his head, pulling him back to his senses. He held his breath, but panic took over. His fellow passengers looked lifeless in their seats, Stan closed his eyes and prayed.

Suddenly a pair of hands had thrust in through the smashed bus window.

The young Stan was cut free from his seatbelt and he was hoisted out, cold, wet, and terrified at almost dying. He gasped for breath.

He hadn't talked for months afterwards and he had never been the same about travelling since.

As if from nowhere his thoughts of the past were interrupted by a white flash of light burning into his eyes, but he was useless to focus. He drifted back into unconsciousness again and the past came flooding back.

He never did find out who pulled him free of the wreckage. He always meant to track down his saviour and thank them, but it had taken him a long time to pluck up the courage to even venture out after that incident, and by then he figured it was too late anyway.

Everyone but him had perished on that bleak, fateful morning. Stan had survived unscathed, apart for mild concussion that had healed over time.

An electric jolt this time, brought him back from his wandering thoughts, but just as quick the darkness came again and his thoughts continued.

Eventually a bench was erected in their memory at the place where it had happened and the old country road was closed to traffic. Over time it became a bridal path.

A new road had opened on the other side of the river. A safer road, not that it had done Stan any good. It would always be a road less travelled.

Another jolt, a distant pleading voice that sounded like Petra... He tried to call out to her. He felt himself slipping away and then a long, drawn-out hum descended onto Stan as he made his way into oblivion.

7

THE FORKED TONGUE

A thin membrane held Stan captive. He struggled to tear it off but his fingers kept slipping on its slimy coated texture. He pushed into it with all the willpower he could muster and still it held him back. He slid down into a crouched position with his knees up to his chin and let out a pathetic whimper.

The cool, white, glowing light emanating from the other side of the membrane was so tantalisingly close, that Stan could almost feel its warmth.

With one last act of strength and determination, Stan rose back to his feet and punched into it with anger and frustration and finally he punched through the tightly stretched substance. He let out a sound of relief.

The light burst through, as Stan retracted his fist, spurring him on to rip the hole bigger.

He struggled for what seemed like hours, but then had stretched the hole big enough to push both arms through and then his head. He twisted and convulsed the rest of his body until at last he slid his uppermost body through. He kicked off with his legs and with a final burst of energy he flopped out onto the other side.

A figure emerged from the shadows at that point, one wearing a long overcoat that seemed burnt and frayed at the seams. A figure, tall and astute with a striking head of jet black hair.

'Sorry I couldn't help you back there,' the figure said, as it pointed to the now torn wall of membrane. 'I'm Will Last, and we have a lot to talk about.' He offered Stan his hand.

'Who the hell are you? Where am I? What is this place?' Stan replied, grabbing the hand to help him get up. Then he added sombrely, 'Am I dead?'

'All in good time, Stan. Just take a moment and I'll explain all,' Will replied. Then, 'You've been through a lot. You need to answer my question first... What do you remember?'

Stan felt somewhat at ease with this person. He didn't feel alarm or panic as he pondered his response.

'Not much, I had an argument with Petra.' The thoughts washed over him. 'Oh God... I threw something in the river.' Stan recoiled in horror. 'I tried to find out what I had done. I chased after her... something hit me, then that...' Stan pointed shakily to the torn and tattered membrane that flapped lazily around in the breeze. 'What the hell is that?' Stan buried his head in his hands and then, 'What on God's green earth is going on?' he said pleadingly.

'Well firstly, Stan, I can put your mind at rest. You're not dead,' Will said, letting the statement linger.

Stan uncovered his eyes. 'So is this some kind of dream or hallucination?'

'Neither, Stan. You are in fact in a coma and this is all in your mind,' Will said, trying to sound reassuring.

'A coma?' Stan spluttered, trying to sum up a fair and rational explanation. 'So, let me get this straight, I'm in limbo then?' he said, agape.

'Technically, yes,' Will replied. 'A limbo you have created inside your mind. One in which I'd really like to help you escape.'

'Okay. Supposing I believe you for a minute. What are you then? A figment of my imagination?' he said disbelievingly.

'Oh no, Stan. I am very real. I am the voice of reason and doubt. I am the decision maker within, that you come to when you seek help. In short I'm your unconscious self – your Guardian.'

Stan scoffed, 'What, like a Guardian Angel?'

'Angel, no. I haven't earned my wings yet, but maybe that's something you can help me achieve, if I help you in return,' Will said hopefully.

'This is all very surreal. If you are my unconscious and this is all in my head, then how do I know this isn't just the effect of some chemicals affecting my brain?' Stan said, laughing like a maniac.

'Who's to say you're right or wrong, Stan? All I know is I have a purpose. As do you, and if you need my help to wake up from your coma, then we don't have much time regardless.'

'Let me just have some time to process this all.' Stan turned his back to Will and took in his surroundings.

Stan hadn't given it much notice or even heard the roar over the buzzing of the words and the conversation he had been involved in at first, but now as he looked around, he could see that he had emerged into a cave. A wall of membrane at the rear from which he came and to the front a cascading curtain of water that he could not see past. The ground was pitted and pools of water had formed on the cave's floor, formed by splashes from the nearby waterfall.

Sunlight was coming from outside, catching the falling spray as it shone though into the cave, creating a dazzling display of moving, shifting light that danced merrily off the walls and reflections from the pools.

Stan stood mesmerised for a moment, lost in thought. Then he began to walk to the waterfall, allured by the sound and light...

'Hold up, Stan. You don't want to go though there yet!' Will hollered at him.

Stan paused, turning back. 'Why not?' he demanded.

'Because you're not ready yet and I need to finish explaining things to you. The instant you pass through there, you're going to be alone and I can't follow after you,' Will sighed.

'Okay Will, I'm listening. I just want to go home. Back to Petra and the kids,' Stan said, shaking his head in disbelief.

'Good, that's what I want too. Okay, here goes.'

Will started with what seemed like the obvious place to start. The membrane Stan passed through was the barrier separating his awake state from his sleep state, and he could not go back that way, only forward. Stan reasoned it was plausible and asked Will to continue.

The reason it occurred was because a coffin had hit Stan so hard in the chest, and more importantly the head, that a clot had formed in his brain and that had put him in the coma.

If Stan was to gain consciousness and wake from his coma, then he would need to travel through his own mind to the source of the haemorrhage and stop it from spreading. It was the root of all evil, as Will had put it.

Stan interjected. 'So what does this, I mean, my clot, look like?'

Will replied that it could take on any manifestation that Stan's imagination could dream up. He wasn't sure what it would present itself as.

Will then proceeded to explain that there was an Oasis of Hope that Stan would be summoned to at some point during his journey. He likened the place to the Thalamus within the brain, which acted as a gatekeeper for messages to pass between the spinal cord and the cerebral hemisphere.

The ominous presence that resided and could be communicated with there, was Thalamus itself. If Stan was to have any hope of returning to reality, then it was prudent that the haemorrhage did not spread there, for it would be game over for Stan and his soul would ebb away to die in reality.

Will explained that Stan's brain was at war with itself and that in order to survive the ordeal, he would need to travel to hell to the blood clot that had formed, and fight his inner demon and win. Again, the manifestations that would present themselves would be the conjuring of Stan's own imagination. Only then would he return to Petra and his two daughters.

'Wait,' Stan exclaimed. 'There's too much information to take in here. You're saying that I need to travel in my own psyche through hell and destroy the clot from within?'

'What you call your psyche, I call the astral plane, but yes, that's exactly what I'm saying. It won't be easy. There are legions that will try and stop you. I refer to them as soul stealers. If you are hijacked by them, then you risk being tainted and again, that's not good for you.' Will stopped and turned his ear to the waterfall. 'We haven't much time left together, Stan,' he added uneasily.

Stan stood in silence.

'Listen, if you become braindead, then potentially you could be stranded in limbo for what would feel like eternity. The surgeons that are keeping you alive at this point could decide to shut down your respirator if you show no signs of recovery and you will die. If you haven't defeated your demons, then you will go to hell.'

'Then this seems pointless. I am doomed to fail,' Stan replied.

'Not if you overcome your phobia, Stan, no. Besides, there is something else that can help you. Something that will help you in your time of need. Something that you have been assigned to help your cause. I was not told its importance, but can only presume it will turn the tide of war in our favour. Strangely enough, it has manifested here into something I think you will relate to.'

Will walked up to the cascading water and reached in. Stan looked on, bewildered, as Will plucked something from within it. Stan looked on in utter astonishment as Will produced from within it a kitten. 'Not exactly a rabbit in a hat, but I think you will recognise this?' he said.

'What is that?' Stan said, alarmed.

Will held him out at arms' length. 'This is the poor unfortunate creature that you unwittingly drowned today down at the river, Stan. This handsome little fellow is going to be your new best friend. Where you go, he goes, but I warn you – if anything happens to him then failure is imminent. This is your sin, but also your salvation,' Will said with a half-smile creeping across his face.

Realisation dawned on Stan. Dumbfounded, he just nodded.

'I've taken the liberty of naming him Heparin. I was going to call him Bobbin, on the count of when I first met him, he was bobbing along the river, but I figured that would be cruel. So "Heparin" is more apt. All I know is that he will help eradicate the clot in you. So long as you can get him to his destination.'

'So you were there too, at my side before this?' Stan said, butting in and sounding perplexed.

'Like I said, Stan, I am your Guardian and I am very real. If you do not succeed, then the ramifications for anyone trying to pass over will also be affected. You need to see the bigger picture. What happens in your head will affect not just you, but all others that follow, even though their stories play out different in their own minds before they pass.'

Stan took the kitten from Will and just studied the tiny ball of fur. 'So how do you know so much and why is this falling on me?' he remarked as he stroked the kitten's fur.

'That, I cannot tell you right now, Stan, but I urge you to trust me,' Will said, aloof.

Stan wasn't too sure.

'Anyway, beyond that wall of water, Stan, is a deep descent into a pool that breaks off into two rivers at a forked tongue. To the right is salvation, to the left your own personal hell, the latter of which is the path you must take. Do you understand?' Will asked.

Stan approached the cascade with the kitten under his arm. 'I think so, yeah. There's just one big flaw in your grand plan, Will.'

'...That is?'

'I'm a hodophobic!' Stan shouted. 'Or did you forget? I'm afraid to admit it. I'm scared to travel, even here!' Stan exclaimed.

'You will be responsible for your own cure, Stan, and besides, I can't see it being a problem,' Will retorted.

'...And why is that?'

'Because you don't have a choice in the matter?' Will said.

Without warning he pushed Stan forcefully through the curtain and out into his untimely fall.

8

THE VIRCHOW'S TRIAD

Three forms stepped out from the gloom of the tower's raised portcullis. A heavy mist greeted them as they stepped out onto the lowered bridge.

The wooden bridge creaked and groaned as the trio made their way across in single file. Occasionally the figures had to sidestep missing boards, and step over protruding ones.

The bridge spanned across a lake, forming a moat around the tower. The mist skimmed the surface of the water that ebbed gently against the side of the bridge, before branching off out in all directions. This created a network beyond.

The head of the trio, Venous, stepped through the mist and out into a burnt, charred, barren landscape that became crispy underfoot.

She stopped and turned round to face her brothers in arms, halting their procession.

'Endo. Hyper. Wait here! I need to make sure the way is clear before we proceed,' she ordered.

Venous was fashioned in strong armour that had been dipped in fresh blood and clad her body, creating a tight but mobile flexing bond. Her long, flowing black hair cascaded down over a kite shield strapped to her back. The shield was rounded at the top and tapered at the bottom and bore a logo of a trident.

She marched on ahead and surveyed her surroundings. The charred black ground she walked upon criss-crossed a deep gorge of lake that stemmed from the moat. It peeled away to meet a lush, green, vibrant meadow on the horizon. In the far distance rolling hills gave way to jagged mountains and through the middle there cut deep fissures containing connecting streams and lakes, that branched off in various directions.

Venous knew the endgame was finally upon them and the battle would soon be won. The newcomer had arrived.

She had sensed the newcomer, as they all had, the moment he arrived and her mission was to intercept this foreign interloper and bring him back to her master, Thrombus, for interrogation.

Checking the skies were clear of winged attackers and that the path ahead posed no concerns, she beckoned over her brothers.

Hyper made it over to her first; standing at just over three feet tall, he was the shortest of the trio but also the fastest. He was clad in the same armour Venous had, but he had a rounded shield that also bore the trident and hung lazily on his shoulder. He had no discernible features as his head and face were burnt beyond all recognition.

Endo was the last to approach. At seven feet tall and rippling with muscle under his armour, he was the most opposing figure. His crew-cut hair was dyed in the fresh blood from fallen foes that had been defeated at his hands. He swung his kite that was strapped to his arm back and forth as he caught the other two up.

Venous smiled at her brothers as they stood before her. No one had ever matched or bested them. They were unstoppable! They were her brothers and together the three of them formed the Virchow's Triad.

Hyper unhooked a whip that was attached to the waist of his armour and shook his shield from his shoulder. It dropped with a heavy clang to the floor. He looked to Venous for assurance.

'Yes my brothers, mount your shields and unhook your whips. Our journey must be fast and our actions swift,' Venous said as she began to mirror Hyper.

Facing the horizon with his comrades, Endo did as his leader requested and flung his shield face down into the dirt. He pushed his left foot into the strapping that would otherwise brace his shield to his arm and took stance on the shield with his right. Unhooking his whip, he gave it a gentle flick and it uncoiled before him, revealing a split fork. At its end was attached a free-spinning disc that protruded from it. Three sharp, pointed, and hooked spikes pierced into the ground, creating a firm hold as it snaked out to the ground before him.

In a "V" formation with Venous at the helm, they all pulled up the slack of their whips. In doing so, the discs spun in the soil and took hold on the spikes, lurching the occupants forward. Sliding on their shields as the whips dug in, spinning and pulling them along, and throwing up debris as the trio sped off into the distance.

*

Stan landed with a splash and sank to the bottom of the fast-flowing river. He kicked with all his might and surfaced into the alien landscape. Inhaling air and treading the water, he looked around for signs of Heparin, who had fallen from his grasp when they had descended the waterfall.

True to Will's word, Stan caught sight of the river splitting off into two. The left, fast-flowing and treacherous. The right, calm and inviting.

In a blind panic Stan scanned both ways for any signs of the kitten, remembering Will's warning. The little fella was his only sense of hope.

Stan finally caught sight of him drifting into the calm waters, his little head bobbing at the surface as he swam towards the embankment, a pitiful meow following.

Stan kicked off and began to swim towards the direction Heparin was making for, but the undercurrent kept pulling him back. Stan realised that the river was too strong as it sent him chasing down into its rapids, leaving the speck of the kitten behind.

Eventually the flow of the river began to slow and Stan found his inner strength return. He swam his way over to some nearby reeds and found his footing in a shallowed outcrop. He grasped hold of some overhanging tufts of grass at the riverbank's edge and hauled himself up.

Rolling onto his back, Stan breathed a sigh of relief and looked at the passing clouds above heralding in the night sky.

A voice echoed in the distance, alerting Stan to his senses. He pulled himself to his feet and looked warily around, trying to make out the direction it was coming from.

Getting his bearings, Stan looked back up the river from the way he came and knew he had to backtrack to find Heparin.

With a great sense of urgency and not wanting to find out who or what the approaching voices belonged to, he broke into a half-hearted sprint towards the kitten's last known whereabouts.

As he approached the split of the river Stan shouted in a hoarse whisper, 'Heparin? Heparin? Where are you, kitty?' He dared not shout too loud for fear of giving himself away.

He decided to follow the contours of the river, as the open ground didn't reveal the kitten in plain sight.

Further along the route he chose, Stan noticed that the river snaked up through a looming valley of large, jagged rocks on either side, clouded by a dark fog that hovered between them. The descending dark was falling too quick and Stan was worried that the kitten may be swallowed up by the darkness.

Just then, more voices came, carried on the breeze from behind him. They were getting closer.

Stan caught sight of the kitten in the distance, who by this point looked to be stationary. As he made his way towards the kitten, he realised the valley was almost upon them.

Heparin, who was cleaning his fur with his tongue, looked up to the approaching Stan, stopped cleaning, gave Stan a wink, then as if undisturbed began to groom himself again.

Just stay there and let me get to you, little guy, Stan thought as he neared with open arms. He reached down and scooped the kitten up, a hand under each of the front paws. But no sooner had he done so, the kitten hissed at him and swiped at Stan's face.

Reeling in shock and surprise, he dropped the kitten, who landed on all fours and retreated for the valley in a swift, terrified panic.

Just as Stan went to give chase a needle-like, hot, searing sensation thrust into his back, bringing him down to his knees. Then as the pain coursed through him, in an instant he was yanked backwards, screaming in agony, into the dark night.

*

'Well, well, boys. Look what we've got here,' Venous cackled, as she dragged Stan, kicking and yelling behind her.

She flicked her wrist with the handle of the whip and the barbed end released from Stan's back. He laid there writhing in pain.

Venous' two companions unhooked their feet from the stirrups and scooped up their shields, returning them to carry positions.

'So, Stanley Palmer. It looks like your journey has come to an end. It must be a relief knowing that it has so. At least now you don't have to relive the nightmares of your phobia,' she said, grinning.

'Who are you?' Stan screamed in terror as he lay twitching at their feet.

'I'm Venous. That there is Endo and over there is Hyper,' she said, pointing to her kin. 'We are the Virchow's Triad and together with your help, we are going to defeat Thalamus at the Oasis.'

'You're insane,' spat Stan as he looked up at his attackers. 'I'll never help you destroy my own mind,' he said between painful breaths as he scrabbled backwards.

'We've been laying dormant here too long, Stanley. Now the battle has shifted in our favour, we will spread out across this land and seize it for our own. You're too far gone to oppose us,' she sneered.

Endo intercepted Stan and forced him to his feet. He wrapped his arms around him, crushing him in the process.

Stan let out a gasp and tried to squirm free, but his captor was too powerful. He felt overwhelmed.

Venous walked up to Stan and thrust a bony finger into his chest. 'Right now your body is being kept alive by machines. It is only a matter of time before they decide to switch it off and you will have no choice but to accept your fate!'

'If I was alone then I'd agree,' Stan said through gritted teeth, realising too late that he had said too much.

Venous circled Stan and coiled her whip, thinking about his revelation. Then she said abruptly, 'William Last!'

She passed behind Endo.

Stan winced. She knew about Will. He hoped she didn't know about Heparin.

'Will won't help you, Stan. This whole sorry mess was his doing after all. He's only in this for one thing. That reminds me, do you have it?'

'Have what?' Stan exclaimed, trying to hide knowledge of Heparin.

'The key. Do you have it?'

'I don't know what you're on about,' Stan said, trying to wriggle free.

'William Last is looking for a key and said you might have it,' Venous said, boring her eyes deep into his.

'You're a liar,' Stan said as he slumped, defeated.

'I think it's time you learned the truth, Stan,' Venous said as she came round again. Stan straightened up, trying to be defiant. 'Ready him for transportation, Endo. We have a change of plan.' Endo nodded and threw Stan over his big, bulking shoulders.

Hyper shot Venous a troubled look.

'It's okay, Hyper. We can afford to wait. Stanley Palmer needs a reality check, so we're taking him back to see Thrombus. The Oasis can wait for now.'

Hyper gave Venous a nervous smile, then went to help Endo secure their passenger for the ride.

'I'm not going to lie, Stan,' Venous said, 'but this next part is going to hurt a bit.' She smiled.

Stan didn't have any time to argue, as Endo threw him down onto his back in a daze, knocking the breath out of him.

Venous threw her shield to the ground and jumped on. She uncoiled her whip and flicked it to the ground ahead. Endo jumped on his shield too, but he flailed his whip at Stan. It uncoiled and wrapped around his legs, binding them tight, and the speared barbs at the end snaked off and embedded into Stan's chest.

The last thing Stan saw just before he blacked out to the searing pain, was Hyper lasso his companions around the waist to form a tether. He then jumped onto his leader's back and Stan could have sworn that he also caught a glimpse of something else. A dark, long, winged creature skimming in and out of the clouds high above. Then darkness took hold.

At last they were off. Surfing out into the darkened night, onwards to the Tower of Thrombus. The very haemorrhage that imprisoned the coma Stan in the hospital and the unconscious Stan in his mind.

High above, a winged entity decided to make his move.

9

THE VALLEY OF LOST SOULS

Lysis had been darting in and out of the cover of black clouds for some time, planning his next move for a daring rescue. He cursed himself for arriving too late.

His first thought was to swoop down and scoop up the kitten the moment it escaped Stan's clutches, but he knew he would have left himself exposed to the silent advancing trio at Stan's rear flank. If he'd timed it wrong then they would have overwhelmed him too, no doubt.

The kitten was safe for now at least, but for how long he could not measure. Those that ventured into the Valley of Lost Souls, rarely returned. But Lysis knew they didn't always have him at their side, and he had on many occasions traversed its deep, foggy descents and come out the other side unscathed.

Lysis was used to flitting above the ominous fog that hovered over the valley, his eyesight keen to see through its thick blanketed state. Many times he had dived down into the swirling black threshold and plucked up unfortunate souls that had wandered in, lost and aimless. This was his secondary purpose. To steer pure souls through unharmed and out to paradise. His first purpose, however, was to wipe out the trio before they spread and took hold of the Oasis. But he hadn't planned on Stan getting captured by them without possession of the key. He figured the key to be a talisman and would aid Stan, he just wasn't sure how, but he was told it was urgent it be delivered safely. *This changes everything,* he thought.

Thalamus had entrusted Lysis with the gilded key in the shape of curved wings, that he was told to give to Stan. The purpose of the key remained a mystery to Lysis, though, but he was told it was of the highest importance. Slipping the key from his pouch hanging from his abdomen, he turned it over in his sticky padded hands.

The gilded key shone bright in the moonlit sky, revealing a fusion of cross-connection veins that spread out to the tips of the wings. They were joined at the middle by a symbol of a circle within a circle, that sprouted eight triangular points around it. A symbol of hope.

Lysis studied the key in his palm, trying to work out its significance. Its wings resembled that of his own, although his were six feet in length and were green in colour, with black patchy markings throughout. These were pure white and translucent and only two inches across.

His wings beat rapidly at his back as he hovered there, surveying the landscape network of rivers below. He returned the key to the pouch and flexed his four limbs. The hairs on them bristled in the wind.

Using his large globular eyes with their 360-degree

vision, he tracked the targets below and with a giant flex of his hard, ribbed, elongated torso that sprouted three spikes at the end, Lysis the giant ten-foot Coffin Fly took flight after his prey.

*

The caravan sped along. The occupants on their shields glided along, bouncing off mounds and ruts of the uneven terrain, dragging their limp captive behind.

Hyper clung on around his master's neck for dear life. The course of action they were taking did not sit well with him. He felt uneasy at his master's decision and became more wary by the minute.

He heard a humming sound emanating from his left and looked to its source. The caravan he was in followed alongside one of the networks of rivers, and as he looked upon the reflection of the moon and clouds on its surface, a winged assailant appeared.

Hyper let out a croaked warning through his melted lips. 'Shhommethhing ishh commming.'

Venous looked over her shoulder and saw it too, but was too late to react. 'Noooo!' she screamed in defiance.

The winged creature that skimmed the river pulled up over the raised bank and sank its head low. The humpbacked arch of its abdomen collided with Endo, who was blissfully unaware of what was happening. He went sailing off into the abyss of the fast-moving surface, sending his shield flying, his grasp wrenched from the whip that dragged Stan along.

Venous turned sideways on her shield, forcing herself to turn. 'Endo!' she raged.

The large Coffin Fly caught Endo's shield in mid arc and flung it sideways at Hyper, knocking him from his master's perch and off into the river.

Venous leapt from her shield and used the tethered whip to somersault into the air.

Lysis, circling back low and snatching up Stan's lifeless body, was making for the skies when Venous grabbed the whip's handle that swung loose from Stan's legs.

The binding Venous had of the tether from her whip to the ground stretched tight and she took up the slack of the whip's loose end tied around Stan, pulling Lysis back from his ascent, bringing him backwards to earth. He brought his limbs close up tight around Stan and brought his wings in to shield them as they went crashing into Venous and all of them went tumbling into a nearby thicket.

Lysis recovered first and using one of his foot pads, or pulvilli, as he referred to them, he grabbed hold of the whip where it met the spears that dug into Stan and used the adhesive quality of his pad to yank them out.

Venous rolled off her back and called out to the dark, 'Hyper, I need you now!'

Hyper was thrashing about in the river; he kept going under the surface as he battled to stay afloat. Venous heard his muffled cries for help, but she knew the threat was not over, she could not aid her fallen comrade.

She glared at Lysis as she retrieved her whip. 'You! Your time ends now! I will finish you off myself!'

She pulled her whip taut and flung it over Lysis' head, trying to garrotte him.

Lysis beat his magnificent wings and took to the sky, trying to shake her loose, but she held firm. As he levelled out, she took astride of his back and pulled tighter on the reins that she had created.

*

Stan regained consciousness and looked around, dazed. The pain in his chest subsiding, he looked around to get his bearings and saw the spectacle in the clouds above. He rubbed his chest and pushed his fingers into the fresh wounds. He winced at the damage he had been inflicted.

Screams overhead stung his ears, as he caught sight of a winged creature barrel rolling in the skies, trying to throw off its enraged occupant.

Stan then heard the splashing from behind and gently rose to his feet. *What the hell is going on?* he thought.

He made his way to the river's edge and peered in. He saw Hyper thrashing about. Hyper pleaded with Stan. 'Hellp mee, pleashhe!' he gasped between mouthfuls of water.

Stan realised now was his time to escape. 'You've gotta be joking!' he shouted to Hyper, and looked back across the bleak, dark landscape.

Seeing the valley in the distance reminded him of his pledge to Will to protect the kitten. With no hesitation, Stan knew that it was time to make a break for it.

Just as Stan began his run, a large hulking figure honed into view from the darkness. It was Endo. He blocked Stan's escape route and bore a wicked smirk.

*

Lysis felt the bind around his neck getting tighter, his vision was clouding and he fell into freefall.

The villainous, vile woman on his back screamed as she clung on.

Lysis picked Stan out below and could see through his blurry vision that he was in trouble. The ground fast approaching, Lysis fanned out his wings and levelled off into a glide. With a final act of vengeance, he bowed his head and flicked up his tail.

Venous was catapulted from Lysis' back and was hurled upside down into the great brute that was Endo. Lysis soared overhead and spun out of control into the path of Hyper drowning in the silky black river.

Hyper flung out his arms and grabbed onto Lysis like a leech just as the Coffin Fly corrected himself and banked hard to the skies once more.

*

Stan seized the opportunity as Venous and Endo lay unflinching in the dirt, and stole up a fallen kite shield and an abandoned whip.

I hope this works for me too, he thought.

Stan threw the shield down, hooked his left foot through the strapping, and planted his right in a stance, trying his best to copy what the kidnappers had done. He cracked the whip. It flailed out and the spinning disc extended the spinning hooked spears into the earth.

The shield lurched into motion immediately as the whip churned up the ground on impact, sending Stan accelerating off towards the waiting valley.

Stan had barely made it to the dark blanket of fog that covered the entrance to the valley, when a low humming noise arose.

The winged creature sailed past him with a limpet attached. Stan recognised the limpet as Hyper, who was trying his hardest to claw away at the creature's ribbed body. For one fleeting moment, Stan thought the winged creature seemed very familiar, but he couldn't fathom why.

The pair rose up above the lingering fog and then momentarily hung lifeless above its ceiling. Suddenly, the winged creature let out a terrible roar and fell, motionless, with Hyper still attached, down into its thick canvas.

Stan eyed the wall of fog as he approached and wondered if any souls had survived within. He gulped at the prospect of finding out.

He felt his heart hammering in his throat and his nerves being ripped to shreds by the very thought of entering, but knew that it was better to chance it here than face what he had left behind. He was sure Venous and Endo would pursue him.

He must overcome his worst fears or die trying and right now that meant rescuing Heparin. But what of the winged creature and Hyper? Would he have to face them too?

He wondered how many other souls this place had claimed. How many lives claimed in this valley? This valley of lost souls?

There was only one way to find out.

10

DARK MATTERS

Stan didn't know how long he had been enveloped by the fog in the valley, but it felt like hours.

The river he followed in through the base had long petered out, leaving only a narrow trickling stream strewn with pebbles and small rocks.

He sat poised on a large boulder in his dishevelled suit and played with the coiled whip in his hands, acting as a soothing agent to his frenzied mind. The shield was propped up against the boulder beside him.

The last few events scrabbled endlessly around his thoughts. Being thrust out into this decaying world of his mind and struggling in the river, he knew that his sin was drowning the kitten unwittingly, and that was why he had drifted left. He also knew that the kitten was pure and that was why he was guided to the right.

The thought of losing his only hope had kept Stan's phobia at bay. Even when he was abducted, his only thought was that of getting Heparin back.

But now as he sat there running the coil through his fingers, the symptoms had come back. The dizziness made him feel light headed and his legs were shaking uncontrollably. He felt lost and totally isolated. The very thought of finding Heparin and making it out of the valley seemed daunting to him. He had been searching for ages but to no avail. He abandoned all hope as his thoughts grew dark.

Close by, a dislodged rock gave way, sending debris down the sloping incline and splashing into the stream. It snapped Stan from his meditated state. He leapt over the boulder and crouched down, just peering over the top, straining to see through the swirling fog whether someone had lost their footing close by.

True enough, seconds later, a short figure slid down and into view. It was Hyper. He cursed to himself for revealing his position and approached the stream warily. He bent down low and scooped up water to his withered, scalded lips.

Stan cursed himself. He had forgotten to retrieve the shield. He went to reach over to get it, but Hyper looked up, dribbling water from his chin and spotted the kite. Stan bobbed back down and pushed his back to the boulder and pondered his next move, his heart beating loud in his chest.

Hyper came splashing across the stream, looked around, and making sure it was safe to do so, picked up the shield and hooked his arm through.

'Shhtannleey, I know you're out here,' Hyper said through pursed lips.

Stan, too afraid to move, glanced around for an escape route.

'Come on Shhtan, I know you're clossse by. Comme out and face mee,' he said challengingly.

Hyper leapt over the boulder and slammed the shield down onto the ground.

'Don't hide fromm mee, Shhtannleey,' he said menacingly as he cast his gaze up the slope.

Stan had retreated up the steep slope behind the boulder and hugged the nearest tree that jutted out. He saw Hyper making his way up towards him. Without hesitation Stan began to climb the tree. He noted it was a dawn redwood tree, he had seen enough pictures of them in his time. Reaching out and using the branches to hoist himself up, he clutched at his chest. His chest ached from the wounds with every grasp. He could not see the top, as the fog was too dense, but spiralled his way up regardless.

Onwards he climbed, spurred on by his approaching attacker. He figured the tree must span over fifty feet.

Hyper heard Stan's ascent and gave chase. He slung the shield around his shoulder and clambered up after him.

Eventually Stan had reached as high as he could go and let out a long breath. He realised he had cleared the fog's ceiling and was met with an extraordinary vista.

The valley spread out before him. Above the immense fog, Stan could see the tops of nearby redwood trees piercing through the blanket, creating pointed narrow tops, the high rise of the steep slopes on either side looming and hemming him in.

To his dismay the valley continued off into the far distance. He looked back and saw that he hadn't made it as far in as he would have liked.

A branch snapped far beneath him, sending Stan into a blind panic. What followed was a deranged scream that was soon muffled by the thick, fetid fog. He knew it meant trouble. Hyper would be on him in no time at all.

Just then, a crazy thought occurred to Stan. It looked do-able but only if he timed it right. He might be able to whip across to the next tree and swing off of it.

He uncoiled the lethal whip and eyed the neighbouring tree. His lips became moist and his palms became sweaty as he prayed it would work.

With a crack of the whip, the tendrils of spikes went soaring, spinning wildly into the thick branches of the nearby tree. With a stroke of luck, they wrapped round a thick branch and the speared, hooked barbs found a hold.

Without thought for safety, Stan pulled hard on the handle and jumped into the void, just as Hyper reached his position behind him, screaming in frustration.

But it was all in vain, no sooner had Stan made half an arc from his swing, the branch gripping the coiled tendrils snapped, plummeting him down and into the fog once more.

Hyper jumped for joy, sensing what had happened, and made his way back down the tree in haste, feeling elated that victory would soon be his.

*

Lysis slithered through the cold stream. He had retracted his wings for fear of damaging them and dragged himself along on his ribbed undercarriage.

The pain from his ripped abdomen was searing hot. He hoped the stream would heal it, if not cool it. He guessed that the stream through the valley held no healing properties though as it was clear to see it was too tainted. The pain spurred him on regardless, even though it did not diminish.

He pulled himself out of the stream and towards a slope, rolling onto his back to check the wound. It oozed a white ethereal substance, the essence of his very soul. He knew his life force was ebbing away. But to his relief, there was no sign of his attacker. He had obviously got lost as all things here did.

When Lysis finally realised he had picked up yet another hijacker, his thought had been to get far away from Stan and draw the Virchows toward himself. Unfortunately that had changed when the short Triad member called Hyper had leeched onto him unawares.

Hyper started attacking Lysis by ripping at his abdomen, but in the process had disturbed the pouch Lysis wore. When Hyper caught sight of its content, he had whooped with glee that he had found the key they were looking for. Lysis had screamed at the uncovering, but Hyper was relentless. His frenzied strikes bore down on Lysis as they wrestled with the pouch.

Lysis knew he had to get the key to Stan at any cost and had decided to cut him off in the valley, but first he had to eject his unwanted passenger.

As they reached part way in, Lysis rose high above the fog and stopped beating his wings. He caught sight of Stan and hoped he would have the sense to track him. They went into freefall, plummeting down into its dark belly. Hyper let go in shock and fell from Lysis, hurtling headlong into a canopy of branches.

Lysis, however, spread his wings at the last minute and glided off out of sight to a safe distance, until the fight went out of him. He skimmed the stream and made contact with a fallen log.

So here he now was, helpless and alone, another victim claimed by the valley.

He didn't know how long he lay there but he kept falling in and out of consciousness for what seemed like aeons.

The next time he came to, he was aware that he was not alone. A small furry creature was sat on his abdomen and was licking at his wound. When it sensed that Lysis had awakened, it stopped licking him and began to preen itself.

The kitten had found him, and somehow Lysis knew he had been part healed by the moggy. Incredibly, the small furry creature was nursing him back to health.

It began to all make sense at once for Lysis; the kitten's purpose became transparent. It had taken on the form here as an innocent animal but the real reason for its presence was much, much more.

Excitedly, he knew he had to take action and be swift in doing so. By some small fortune he had now acquired two keys, the winged key and the kitten. He hoped Stan was alright, because now, they held all the keys to the future.

*

Stan saw Hyper approach through the swirling fog with his shield raised. He struggled to get to his feet, but he was still too winded to move properly. He reached for the handle of the whip lying by his side and swung it blindly at Hyper. The talons at the end of the whip still gripped onto the branch that they had broken free.

The branch made contact with the shield and on impact shattered into chunks of flying bark, releasing the branch's remnants from the talons' grip.

Hyper circled Stan slowly and retreated back into the fog only to re-emerge seconds later, ever closer.

Stan flailed the whip again. This time, now free of bark, the talons struck the kite shield causing sparks to fly from the metal contact. Stan got quickly to his feet.

Again, Hyper retreated into the shrouded darkness. Stan yanked back on the whip and grabbed hold of the disc. The sharp steel barbed knives protruded from its outer edge.

Stan backed off into the fog himself, hoping it would give him some camouflage and even the playing field.

A flash of steel emerged and rammed into Stan, knocking him back. He cursed and spun round, looking for Hyper. Again, it came. This time Stan was ready. He dived to his left and thrust his hand up, feeling the knives slice into their mark.

Hyper howled and disappeared from view. It spurred Stan on as he gave chase. A flash of steel again, this time it made contact with Stan's shoulder and sent him spinning into the stream. Then Hyper was upon him, smashing the shield over and over into Stan's body and snatching back the whip.

Stan thought he was surely done for, but then something unexpected emerged from the fog. In a flash a pair of arms extended out and grabbed hold of Hyper, surprising them both. Hyper screamed as the darkness consumed him, and he was hauled off out of sight.

Deathly silence followed, leaving Stan alone and badly shaken. His body numb from the beating and his chest and back still painful from the lashes, not knowing who or what had taken Hyper and if he would be next, but also relieved that he had been spared for now at least. He just hoped that what had helped him would not come back to claim him too.

Stan didn't know how long he had stood there frozen to the spot, but when nothing else happened he turned and made his way deeper into the valley.

*

It was some time later that Stan became uneasy and restless again, when a small pair of eyes blinked at him from a hollow of a tree.

He didn't know whether to run or hide but curiosity got the better of him. He approached the hollow and found to his surprise, Heparin staring back up at him.

Euphoria took hold of Stan. 'Heparin, thank God, I've found you,' he said, welling up.

'No, Stan, I would say that it is we, who have found you,' a voice exclaimed from behind him.

Stan jumped forward in fright and turned around,

his jaw dropped.

Before him, perched on a fallen log, was a giant fly-like creature. It had big, blue, bulbous eyes and its body was long and elongated with black and green striped ribs running down to a three-pronged tail. The fly extended its magnificent shimmering wings, they shone brightly in the faint moonlight.

Stan blurted out to his own amazement, 'I've seen you before, you were in my comic when I was a child.'

'Yes you have, Stan. "The incredible Coffin Fly". My name is Lysis and I am at your service,' he exclaimed as he bowed his head. Stan was struck dumbfounded. This thing could talk too!

Plucking up the courage, Stan asked, 'Was it you that pulled Hyper into the fog and rescued me just now?' He caught himself stammering.

'No, but whoever did was clearly playing advocate, Stan.'

'I, I guess so,' Stan exclaimed.

'Well anyway Stan, now we've found you, we must all be going,' the thing called Lysis hummed.

'Going where?' Stan said.

'You'll see, Stan, but we have much to discuss as we fly. I suggest you pick up the kitten and climb aboard,' Lysis said as he swung his tail round to Stan, offering Stan to climb on.

'You're not seriously expecting me to go on a flight with you, are you?' Stan exhaled.

'You must, Stan. We are not safe here and besides,

you don't look like you could walk much further. You look more beaten up than me. So let's make haste, shall we?' Lysis' wings began to thrum rapidly, as they flicked up and down.

Stan scooped up Heparin and climbed warily onto Lysis' back. 'OK. Here goes, Heparin,' he said as he made his way over.

The Advocate, as Lysis had named him, looked on from the shadows. He knew now what he must do.

He turned his back and retreated into the black abyss.

11

THE ADVOCATE AND THE EMBOLI

The Advocate made his way back to the prisoner. Falling short of revealing himself to the immobile captive, he remained behind the veil of the fog.

Hyper was bound at the ankles by the whip's talon ends that were strung up high over an arching branch and ended at a trunk of a tree, knotted by the handle around its thick roots. His unconscious body swung back and forth, a short-distance gap between his head and the ground.

Reaching down into the stream nearby, the Advocate picked up a handful of wet, shiny pebbles and pushed them around his palm. Looking for one that seemed to have the sharpest edges, he winced as the gravel seeped into his scarred hand.

On selecting a pebble with a fine edge he retracted his arm and launched it free from his grasp in a forward thrust. The projectile hit Hyper in the face but caused no reaction. Fuming, he abandoned the remaining pebbles and kicked over a rock. Picking it up, he did the same again. This time the stone hit

Hyper in a freshly sliced open wound at his shoulder, below where his armour had exposed the flesh.

Hyper's eyes flashed open immediately and he began to writhe in agony.

'Where is the key?' the Advocate demanded.

'I donnt havvve iit,' Hyper bawled.

'LIAR, you had the opportunity to retrieve it, now where is it?'

Hyper swung in a lazy arc. 'I failed to gett itt, but I found Sttannleey insstead.'

'THAT was not the deal we had. You were told to leave him unharmed for now.'

'Venous got impatient. We did not knoow where thhe key wass, jusst the locationn of Shhtan. We were going to ennd the war annd deliveer himm to Thhrommbuss.'

'I told your master where he would be in order to spy on him. Once Lysis had shown up and given him the key, then you could apprehend Stan, but only when Lysis had gone and Stan became vulnerable.'

'Wee thought that hee already had itt,' Hyper wailed.

'Well you thought wrong. Now they have joined up together... I still want THAT key!'

'Lysis has it in a pouch on his person.'

'You better pray that is so.'

Hyper sensed the Advocate venture off into the mist. 'Donn't leeave mee!' he wailed after him.

The Advocate returned moments later, dragging behind him a large branch that was on fire.

'Oh, I'm not going to leave you. In fact, I'm going to take you to your mistress... but I will make a further example of you first,' he said.

Hyper saw the branch ablaze and pleaded with the Advocate. 'Pleasse, I do ass you ask. Let me go.'

The branch was dragged into view and placed directly below Hyper's squirming body. The arc of the fiery glow illuminated his armour.

The Advocate took hold of Hyper's head and held it steady. Charred black flakes came away from his scalp as the heat began to centralise at his crown.

'I'll do anything you want. Anything!' Hyper pleaded.

'I know you will. Funny, ain't it?'

'What is?' Hyper screamed, as his head began to blister.

'Funny that when you're under pain or stress, that voice of yours becomes... well... normal.'

The Advocate pushed Hyper, who then began to swing backwards and forwards, causing Hyper to scream with each passing of the flames that licked into the sky.

'I punished you before when you betrayed me to Venous. At least now I will have her full cooperation... and she won't have the chance to do this to me again,' the Advocate said as he showed his semi-healed palm to Hyper.

'I will show you and your brother, Endo, where the Oasis is and how to breach it. In return Venous can fetch me the key herself because it seems you're useless at achieving anything.'

'Yes, I will do as you ask.'

'Good, because this is the last time I play Advocate to Thrombus, do you hear me?'

'Yes, yes. Please let me go,' Hyper warbled as the top of his head caught alight.

The Advocate strode over to the roots where the handle of the whip was bound and turned to look at Hyper. With a swift stomp he kicked through the roots, causing the whip to unravel. Hyper went screaming headlong into the fiery branch.

Kicking and screaming, Hyper was set ablaze as the flames engulfed his body. The Advocate then reached down and grabbed the handle before dragging the burning Hyper off to the entrance to the valley.

*

Venous and Endo stood waiting as instructed by the Advocate, at the entrance to the valley. Too fearful to enter its dark domain.

At last, the Advocate greeted them, dragging behind him the crispy, charred, smoking Hyper.

Venous stood with her hands on her hips and sneered at the advancing party.

'He had better not come to any harm,' she said, pointing at her blackened brethren.

'He will be fine, but heed my warning, Venous. If you do not deliver the key I seek then you shall be forever lost in this limbo,' retorted the Advocate.

'Oh come now, William Last. You may have bested Hyper but you don't surely think that you can get one over on me, do you?' she challenged.

'That winged key is my chance to escape this realm that I have been denied for so long. If Stan realises what he now possesses then I will not get my wings and he will return to reality. It is in both our interests to stop that outcome materialising,' Will said, as he bent down to untie the bind from Hyper's ankles.

Venous retorted, 'You are already tainted, William, I saw to that when I lashed your palm. Your fate will be the same as Stanley Palmer's, who I'd like to add has also been tainted by my hand.'

'I care not what happens to Stan. When I have the key I will be long gone and you can consume his entire mind for all I care! So would you like me to hand over Thalamus to you in exchange for the key or not? Do we have a deal?'

'Yes, we have a deal.'

'I trust you to get me the key, Venous, and only you. I will take Endo and Hyper to the secret location of Thalamus at the Oasis and you can return to you master, Thrombus, which is where Stan and Lysis are heading to.'

'You mean to tell me that they are headed there now?' she barked.

'I give you that information as a gesture of goodwill. So I suggest you run along to your master now, Venous,' Will said as he coiled the freed whip around his knuckles.

'Does Stanley Palmer know that the key he has, is the key to his salvation?' Venous said as her fallen comrade came to.

'No, he does not and it shall remain that way. He

thinks it will destroy Thrombus, as I have led him to believe,' Will said mischievously.

'Very well, then you promise me no harm will befall my master?' she shrieked.

'I promise no harm shall come of it. It is a fool's errand I assure you,' Will said, flashing her a smile.

'One last thing before I go, William Last...' She let the statement linger.

'Yes, Venous,' he sighed.

'We all have our purpose here in this astral plane of Stanley's mind, but I have yet to figure out yours,' she pondered.

'As of now my purpose has changed. I am no longer Stan's Guardian but more of the Emboli that seeks to keep him here so I may flourish elsewhere,' Will said knowingly.

'Then pray that our paths do not cross again, Emboli, for although our goals are different, both will have the same ending,' she said.

'Oh, I'm counting on it,' Will said. 'I'm counting on it,' he repeated.

12

ON WINGS AND A PRAYER

Lysis stole through the brightening sky. His wings hammered against the cool breeze emanating from the east that brought the sun into focus. He dipped down low and caught an updraft, sailing them up higher into the heavens.

'Look all around you, Stan. Isn't it wonderful, this world you have created in your mind?'

'I feel sick,' Stan said as he gripped on tighter with his eyes closed.

'Heparin does not agree, Stan! Look at him, he looks quite calm up here catching the wind in his fur,' Lysis said, as he stole a look to his back.

Stan had quite forgotten all about Heparin once they had taken flight and risked a glance to see what he was doing.

Heparin was wrapped tight by Lysis' forked tail and hung motionless between them. He was washing his face with his paw and paid no attention to where he was.

Stan laughed. 'He doesn't know any better for how it feels to be afraid of travel.'

'Yes, he had no time to experience fear or life...' Lysis trailed off.

'You're right, Lysis. I feel so ashamed. He doesn't deserve what I have done to him.' Stan felt his eyes begin to well up.

'I'm sure whatever fate had in store for you, befell him too. Your paths are tied together for a greater purpose.'

'Still doesn't explain my actions though. My phobia got in the way as usual,' Stan said glumly.

'You can't be stuck in the past, Stan. You must embrace your future and begin to live life in the moment,' Lysis said with an optimistic tone.

Stan opened both eyes and looked around the landscape, his tears whipped away by the breeze.

Hills and forests rolled by below, green and vibrant, not yet touched by the coming darkness. Wild flowers sprouted in meadows, adding to the eclectic mix. A wild assortment of kaleidoscopic colours that spread far and wide.

A network of rivers branched out in several directions and followed the lay of the land.

'It's beautiful!' Stan shouted above the hum of Lysis' wings and the distorted wind that had built up. 'This is how I perceive my mind?' he stated.

'Yes Stan, this is the place your mind dreams up when you are relaxed or in need of getting away from the harsh realities of life. Your own personal sanctuary, that no one can invade.'

'But I guess it can turn quite dark too when I experience times of trouble?'

'Yes Stan, but a haemorrhage can be fatal of much more! Just look to the horizon, the damage is catastrophic!'

Stan saw a dark veil in the distance; lightning flashed from its core.

'We're heading there aren't we? We're heading to the very root of my condition.'

'I will drop you as close as I can, Stan, but I cannot follow you all the way. I have to fight your personal battle elsewhere in order to give you a fair chance of succeeding,' Lysis said as he dropped in altitude.

'Why can't you help me see this through?' Stan said, puzzled.

'All that exist in your mind, Stan, have a purpose. Whether intended or not. My calling is to destroy the Virchow's Triad that created your haemorrhage before they can spread to the Thalamus, rendering you braindead. Thrombus is the haemorrhage that you must destroy so you can wake from your coma and Heparin is the anticoagulant administered into you, to eradicate it completely.'

Stan couldn't believe what he was hearing. 'So Heparin is my cure?' he said, aghast.

'Yes, but I don't know how he is going to deliver yet. You see, it wasn't until I was wounded in the valley, that Heparin came to my aid and by licking my wounds, repaired the damage inflicted by Hyper.'

'So what's he going to do, lick the haemorrhage to death?' Stan exclaimed in utter astonishment.

'Hold on a second, Stan,' Lysis said. He tilted his left wing downwards and circled over to a clearing before coming to a stop mid-flight and hovered above the spot of a meadow. 'Obviously I don't know how he will help you. All I know is that the talons that extend from the Virchow's Triad's whips, taint whatever they touch. So in comparison I can only assume that Heparin works in a similar way.'

'Ok. Supposing what you say is true, then what is Will's purpose in all of this? I mean, he claims to be my Guardian and he gave me Heparin, but since I've arrived here he has been allusive.'

'I do not know of who you speak, but I will find out for you, Stan, if you wish,' Lysis stated.

'Thank you,' Stan said as he craned his neck to look into Lysis' big bulging eyes.

Lysis lifted up one of his padded feet and reached into a pouch. Stan hadn't noticed the pouch before. He gave Lysis a meaningful look.

Lysis pulled out the shimmering winged key and held it out to Stan.

'This is for you, Stan,' he said, offering it up.

Stan turned the winged key over in his hand.

'What is this? It's too beautiful for words.'

'I am afraid I do not know its true purpose, Stan. Only that it was entrusted to me by Thalamus to give it to you only. It must be of some great significance.'

Stan inspected the fine embroiled design and for a fleeting second sensed elation and joy.

'It clearly means something to you, Stan.'

'I, I don't know, it's just a feeling I get from it. A feeling of home.' Stan wept.

'You must keep it secret, Stan, as that short Triad member, that insufferable, hideous charred creature knows that I have it. He has his sights on obtaining it.'

'They must think it's the cure,' Stan said. 'That means they can't know about Heparin. We have an advantage.'

'I hope you're right, Stan,' Lysis said.

'If they think you have it and you're going to face them, then that buys us time to deliver Heparin to the source,' Stan said jubilantly.

'Just be aware though, Stan, in case they guess our ruse. If you're caught now, then we could be in tremendous trouble!'

Stan for once felt elated. It seemed at long last that things were going to be alright for a change.

Stan stowed the winged key in his breast pocket and buttoned it shut. He looked to the horizon with a great sense of triumph and knew his time of courage had come.

Lysis took off again and they made their way to the impending darkness, but for once Stan did not fear travelling into the unknown. In its place he felt something new, he felt hope.

13

SYNAPSE BRIDGE

As Lysis took to the skies once more, he left Stan with some parting advice. Not all is what it seemed, and to be aware that for some souls it is already too late.

Stan, cradling Heparin in his arms, waved a fond farewell to the unusually strange Coffin Fly and turned to face the bleak scene before him.

He stood on the threshold of a rich, colourful, flourishing landscape and a dark, bleak, deadened wasteland. The contrast between the two mirrored the ongoing battle he was fighting, to hold on to his precious life.

He stepped over into the decayed ruins with trepidation and felt the warmth from the charred ground rising up. Ash particles billowed all around.

He looked back to the hope he left behind; the morning sky, a hue of orange with gentle rolling clouds, drifting aimlessly across its surface. The sign of better times. He sighed, inwardly praying that whatever awaited him would not be the stuff materialised of his own nightmares and that he would have the courage to overcome it and save himself.

The thought of not knowing what to do when he arrived at his destination or what he might find, filled him with apprehension and dread.

He stroked Heparin behind the ears and in return the kitten butted his face. Stan hoped that when the time was right, they both might then know what they were to do.

Pressing on, the pair made their way across the desolate surface. Stan noticed blackened stems jutting from the earth and charred bushes devoid of life, where once it had thrived in abundance. He wished evermore for it to return.

Dark clouds drifted into view accompanied by a low, startling thunder. As the duo trudged on, the sky ignited with brilliant white flashes heralding in lightning that forked between the veil of clouds.

Heparin's ears went back in fright and he clawed to get inside Stan's suit jacket. Offering assistance, Stan ushered Heparin inside and cradled his arms so the kitten would not fall through. A soft mew from the creature followed, comforting Stan and making him feel protective of the agitated kitten.

Still they pressed on, but then without warning the sky opened up and rain came lashing down. As it hit the charred remains, it sizzled on contact, the cold, wet droplets not agreeing with the hot offerings of the soil it met.

Stan pulled his lapels up, turning his face into the storm, and continued on.

From out of nowhere he heard a large crack and

looked to its source. A large welt had appeared in the ground and steam escaped from within. Then without warning, it widened into a fissure that split open the ground in front of them. It continued to fork out in many directions at once, revealing a glowing, moving stream beneath.

Realising in horror that it was lava flowing beneath him, Stan broke into a sprint in haste. Some fissures formed behind him in hot pursuit and some overtook him and snaked off across his path. He veered off to the left just in time but was met with a split that opened up from behind him and passed beneath his legs, creating a wide, large chasm before him. Stan ran full pelt at the opening and leapt across, narrowly landing safely across its aft.

In a blind panic he darted across newly forming fissures and tried to keep abreast of those that chased him, leaping at intervals across any that dared stray into his path.

Heparin jostled in Stan's jacket. His little head poked out and he sniffed the air. The smell of sulphur burned his senses and he quickly buried his head again.

Fire began to spew forth from the apertures, sending flames curling into the torrential rain. The very atmosphere crackled and spat as the environmental hazards collided.

Stan shielded his eyes from the blazing eruptions that sprang up around him and twice he nearly lost Heparin, who had slipped down to his waist.

He spotted a long wooden bridge far off into the distance and tried to keep it in his sight as he ducked and weaved towards it. If he could make it there, he thought, then he may have a chance of leaving the infernal obstacles behind.

Another crack echoed in the turmoil. This time hot molten lava spat out fist-sized embers of rock followed by a maelstrom of many more from all the exposed vents, sending them high into the air only to arc and come raining down all around Stan. The rain zapped them and steam billowed off before they hit the ground, disorientating Stan.

The rocks exploded against the ground, sending shards flying in all directions. One came too close to Stan for comfort and made him tense at the thought of what damage they would inflict if he was caught.

It was then he made his error; a nearby rock exploded to his right and caused him to turn away from the flying debris, however, as he did so a fissure opened up underneath him and caught him unawares. He lost his footing and he dived in time to clear it but landed hard on his right shoulder, ejecting poor Heparin from the confines of his jacket, who tumbled out before him.

Before Stan could recover, another rock exploded near his head and he curled up into a ball to protect his face. The debris kicked up soot that blanketed him, but sent Heparin scampering off in terror.

Stan knew they were both in trouble, but sensed he, more than Heparin, was in the gravest danger. He envisioned the fissures of lava, like the network of rivers he had manifested, were actually nerve cells in his brain that carried signals to other parts of his body. But if the rivers were his emotional state of calm, then the lava was the pathways of pain and right now the events that were unfurling before him were not a good indicator of his mental state.

He picked himself up and with all his willpower, pushed on. He could see Heparin getting away from him and heading for the bridge and so he trundled off after him.

*

Eventually Stan made it to the bridge and as if by chance the commotion of the shifting land behind him had begun to quieten again. Stan got his composure back and patted his suit down, sending wisps of charcoal soaring from his suit.

He spotted Heparin up ahead grooming his fur with his tongue. Stan smiled. For all they had endured the kitten sure was resilient and was carrying on as if nothing had happened! There he was halfway across the bridge preening himself.

Stan eyed the bridge suspiciously. It was at least ten feet wide and at least one hundred and fifty feet in length. It spanned across a large body of water, that lapped at the bridge's edges, spilling over in places. A mist hovered above the river, obscuring its murky depths.

Stan got the feeling of dread again and licked his lips. Something seemed off. He looked to the far side of the rickety, wooden bridge and saw a closed portcullis that dwarfed in comparison to the building it was housed in.

As he cast his gaze up the brickwork that housed it, he took in the high rise of a tower for the first time. Its mottled grey stone texture looked impenetrable as it rose from out of the moat to the sky above.

Stan craned his neck and followed the contour of the tower up. It reminded him of the shape of a wolf's fang protruding from a bleeding gum. A sharp point at its summit and the moat circling the tower at its base.

As he took in the visceral image he saw an arched formed window near the point and a soft glow was radiating from within. A dark shadow passed by the window and startled Stan from his mesmerised gaze.

Feeling flustered and somewhat disturbed, Stan looked back to the bridge and shrugged off the feeling of being watched.

He ventured out onto the bridge and was met with the soft creaks and groans of the boards underfoot. Unperturbed, he delicately made his way out.

He had ventured too far, when curiosity got the better of him. He veered off to the edge of the bridge and knelt down. He wafted the mist with his hand to get a better view of the surface and cocked his head. The gentle splashes lapped to and fro but he strained his ears and heard a low murmuring beneath its depths. It was as if the river was coming alive. It sent chills running down his spine and he reeled away.

Heparin stopped cleaning and his ears pricked up; he sensed the low murmuring too.

Stan went to get up, when he caught something moving from beneath a missing board on the bridge. He grabbed hold of the timber edges and peered in. What greeted him was terrifying! Startled and afraid, he began to edge away. A thousand eyes stared back at him in unison.

On seeing him, the murmuring became a cacophony of cries and moans. There were bodies under the bridge, floating in its depths. They became frenzied on seeing Stan and began to scrabble at the underside of the bridge. Clawing and thudding erupted as the bodies began to clamber over one another and tear through the bridge.

Stan looked to Heparin, too petrified to move. The kitten backed away further along.

'No, Heparin, stay where you are,' Stan hissed.

A slimy, grey, decaying hand shot up through one of the planks and splintered it in two. It grabbed hold of Heparin.

'No!' Stan shouted as he lurched towards the kitten.

Everything happened in a blur. The moment Stan raced across the rotten timbers, he gave himself away. The bodies beneath him started to smash their way through. A hand grabbed hold of his ankle and he went down with a crash.

More hands sprang up around him, splintering boards in two. Some boards fell away into the writhing mass where they were dragged down into the throng. Stan tried effortlessly to kick the hand away but another took its place. Then he was restrained. Hands had coursed through and grabbed hold of his shoulder, his waist, his legs, and his head. He looked pleadingly to Heparin.

The kitten hissed at the hand that held it immobile and he swiped at its bony fingers. The grip tightened and Heparin gave out a shrill scream. Then he was gone as the hand yanked him through the hole and out of sight.

Stan looked on in horror and thrashed to get free, but the hands held him steadfast.

The bridge buckled and bowed and the water was thrashed as the writhing mass pulled and pushed and smashed through in a frenzy.

Then the bridge disintegrated. Flotsam and jetsam dispersed in every direction as Stan was hauled off into the abyss.

As Stan joined the fray, the feeling of loss descended over him. He would soon become a victim like the rest of these lost souls, joining them forever in their watery grave.

Time seemed to freeze, as he floated there, interlocked by the plethora of bodies. The water began to dull his senses and the bodies closed up around him, obscuring his vision. The fight went out of him and he was about to give himself over to the inevitable.

But then hope emerged. The bodies holding him began to swim away and the ones closest to him released their grip. Stan, momentarily frozen, began to see an opening. A new vigour surged through him as again he was becoming free.

He kicked and pushed at his captors as they were disappearing off into the darkness and saw a faint glow of white light.

Transfixed, Stan treaded water as the light slowly came into focus. It grew brighter and brighter as if pushing back the darkness, then it circled in a lazy arc and began to drift away. Stan kicked off and swam after it, lured like a moth to a bulb.

As he followed the light, the lost souls that got in its way retracted and vanished into the depths once more. Stan scanned around for Heparin, hoping and praying that he too would catch sight of the light and swim towards it. Onwards Stan swam, closing the gap between himself and the light as he did so.

Eventually the light drifted up towards the surface and Stan found himself momentarily stunned by the light as he hit the edge of the moat's bank.

He came up gasping for air and was glad to see he had made it to the other side. With fear of being pulled under again now the light had gone, Stan pulled himself free and back to dry land. He vowed he was done with water once and for all.

He looked out across to where the bridge once stood and knew his true intent. He would not get back, especially knowing now what lay beneath the surface of the river. There wasn't a hell's chance of braving those waters again, and with no synapse bridge to take him back safely, he knew this was now a one-way trip.

Sitting there, he looked around and saw that he had come up just short of the portcullis. With still no sign of Heparin, he now feared the kitten was gone again and sensed that his only true hope of destroying Thrombus was robbed from him.

He padded his pocket and gave a sigh of relief that the winged key was still buttoned tight. He unbuttoned his pocket and pulled it free. This was all he had to hold onto in this world now. He still didn't know its use but hoped that it would be all he needed. It gave him only a small glimmer of hope.

It was then that the portcullis rose up into the parapet as if reading his thoughts. He cursed the haemorrhage and whatever form it held for thwarting him once more and inviting him in, now knowing that the last of his hope had gone. The kitten, Heparin, lost forever.

14

AXON ASCENSION

Passing through the threshold of the raised portcullis, Stan had to adjust his eyes to the radiating glow that greeted him.

As his peripheral vision returned the portcullis slammed shut behind him, jolting him forward.

Stan looked around and saw that he was stationed in a wide, circular, stoned room with a low-hung ceiling that ran wet with condensation. Drops of water trickled down the walls and leaked from the ceiling.

Glancing down, he noticed he was standing on a large flagstone that was sitting on a hot bed of lava. He then noted more flagstones away from his right that bore off left in an arch that formed stepping stones around a pool. They too sat on the lava. The path seemed to lead to an open doorway at the far end of the room.

Rivulets of water from the ceiling sizzled on the lava's surface and splashed the stepping stones, causing wisps of steam to rise up in the air.

To his left there was the large round pool that was off-centre to the room, housed in a narrow brick lip that separated its contents from the lava. Between himself and the pool lay another flagstone but only half of it was exposed. The other half, hidden by the pool itself.

Wall-mounted fire torches adorned the walls on all sides and were well spaced, completing a ring of fire at eye height. Their hard steel mounts were bolted fast to the slippery, wet walls.

Stan stepped to the half-submerged stone to his left and got a better look of the pool's substance. It looked to be made up of a thick, dark grey, gloopy liquid. Air pockets were forming at the surface, forming stretched bubbles. Some popped and hissed as their air escaped.

Stan turned back, not wanting to linger any further at the thought of what it was, and looked across to the open door across the room. He spotted stone steps through the doorway that seemed to work their way up, spiralling out of sight.

He hesitated briefly and looked at the stepping stones again. Water glistened on their surface and Stan weighed that if he put a foot wrong then he could slip off and into the waiting lava. He had to be cautious when he traversed them or he would meet a grisly fate.

As he made his way across the stones he saw that the path did not end at the doorway but merely passed by it and continued arching left where it met the rear of the pool. It puzzled him as to why it would do so, but his question was quickly answered when the stepping stones began to flow anti-clockwise.

The path began to reverse. Stones that were once visible behind him began to disappear beneath the pool, and off to the rear of the pool new ones emerged.

The movement was slow at first, but with every step forward Stan made, the speed began to increase. The path was drawing him back to the pool, which he knew it would eject him into.

Stan picked up the pace and tried to outrun its momentum but found himself slipping on the stones. With each correction and trying to stay on, the path lured him back more on its roundabout of death.

He started to leap across to get more speed when an all too familiar sound erupted behind him. Grey, lifeless souls rose from the surface of the pool and stared after him, torsos and arms reaching out, baying for his blood.

Stan shrieked in terror and continued his leaps and bounds, but again the path began to spin faster; his energy levels were beginning to waver.

He lost his footing and slid on a flagstone. He fell down onto his knee and the stone took him back further. He had only made it round halfway.

The grey, lifeless souls continued their wailing and all jostled over one another to be the first in line to grab Stan.

Getting back on his feet, Stan pressed on and leapt again, this time he overshot the mark as the stone whizzed by beneath him. He flailed his hands in the air and caught hold of one of the wall mounts containing a fiery torch.

The stones blended into one another in a blur, as Stan looked on. It spun on rapidly and Stan felt himself get dizzy, but he was safe as he hung on to the wall mount, his feet inches from the lava.

The mass of souls cried out in unison as their chance to grab Stan again failed.

Praying the wall mounts would take his weight, as the one he held on to did, Stan began to swing from one to the other. He almost lost his grip on one grab as his hands became sweaty, but managed to hook his arm over.

Finally, with one last jump he swung in through the open doorway and landed in a heap on the floor.

*

Climbing the steep ascent up the stairwell, Stan hugged the outermost wall, occasionally ducking down to avoid the overhead torches that lit the way.

He had come across numerous doors to his left at various levels on his way up, but each time he decided to pass them by.

The silhouette that he had seen earlier, passing the only window he noticed from the outside, was strong in his mind. It was towards the pinnacle of the tower and so Stan knew that was where he must head to meet his destiny.

Water clung on to the steps as he travelled upon them, and dripped down over the sides in mini cascading waterfalls.

He splashed through them and continued on.

More doors, more opportunities to open them up and peer inside confronted Stan, but he resisted the temptation to look, for fear of side-tracking this quest that had been thrust upon him.

As the last of the steps honed into view, Stan passed one more door on his left but unlike the others, this door was ajar. Stan stopped outside and went to reach for the brass rounded handle, but retracted at the last minute.

He carried on up one last bend and the steps ended. A large wooden door barred his way. A blood-soaked handle in a triangular shape protruded from its left.

Again Stan hesitated. His hand hovered over the handle. Sweat and perspiration ran down his back. The fear and dread washed over him again.

A shrill scream from below startled him. A man's voice cried out in pain. Stan knew in an instant who it belonged to, but he couldn't believe it. He sensed it had to be a trap, a false sense of security. It sounded very much like De'Ath Cummings' voice coming from the next floor down.

Stan bounded down the stairs in haste, using his hands on both opposing walls to steady his descent, and made a beeline for the open door. With a slight pause to steel himself, he barged the door wide open and burst in.

He skidded on a slippery surface and fell onto his back, sliding across the floor. Blood was all around him. The floor, ceiling, and walls were coated in it, oozing and pulsating as if he had entered the inside of a beating heart.

He got to his feet, but became unsteady as he slipped and slid around, his suit, hands, and face caked in the rich, crimson substance.

He saw De'Ath and reeled in shock. Nausea rose

from the pit of his stomach as he saw his old acquaintance suspended a few feet in the air. De'Ath was in the centre of the room with a thick vein-like tube extending from his stomach, hanging like some twisted baby's mobile toy suspended above a cot.

White pulsing lights passed from De'Ath and up the vein-like tube that twisted green and blue and disappeared through a hole in the ceiling.

De'Ath's complexion was mottled grey and he looked like his very life force was being drained from him.

Stan, in a blind rage, threw himself at the sinewy vein and yanked as hard as he could, but his hands slipped off its slimy texture.

De'Ath screamed in agony as he was buffeted around, but Stan was relentless. He wrapped his arm around the tether and pulled with all his might. The vein stretched taut and finally it tore, sending De'Ath and Stan to the floor. The torn ends of the vein spat out globules of blood like a severed artery.

'De'Ath, old friend, can you hear me?' Stan shouted, but was met with a low whimper.

Stan pulled De'Ath to his feet and hooked an arm under his shoulder.

'I'm getting you out of here,' he promised.

Stan and the semi-conscious De'Ath made it back out onto the stairwell and Stan looked up and down.

'I don't know a way out, my friend, but I think I'm going to chance going back the way I came. Just bear with me,' he said.

Stan and De'Ath splashed down the steps but had

hardly made it one flight when a step shifted under their feet. Like a domino effect all the steps followed suit and dropped away at a forty-five degree angle, creating a watery spiralling slope.

Their legs gave way and downwards they shot on their backs. Stan knew that once they got through the opening, then the spinning path would take them and send them into the pool at the end. He tried to spread his legs to get traction off the walls, if not stop them, then at least slow their progression, but it was no use; Stan's shoes were bloodied and wet. They hurtled faster on.

As they neared the open doorway, Stan went to close his eyes against what awaited, but just as he was about to he saw a tether was tied across the opening, barely a foot from the ground. Stan grabbed hold of De'Ath around the waist and with his free hand he hooked on to it; they both came to an abrupt stop.

Stan couldn't believe his eyes, but the moment soon passed when he looked out to the stepping stones. They were slowly rounding their way when he saw Venous riding one stone that came to halt in front of them.

'Did you miss me, Stan?' Venous said as she shone a wicked smile. 'Now if you don't mind... Give me the key.'

15

THE PIT OF DESPAIR

The large brute that was Endo marched across the vale, with a charred Hyper hanging off his back.

Will had already vanished into the wild flower pathway, leaving behind instructions for Endo to follow the sound of his whistling.

Listening out for Will's whistles, Endo and co. trundled along. 'Why is it we can't see you or this flowery path?' Endo grunted in a brisk tone.

'I told you, only the pure can find and walk the path to the Oasis,' came the reply from the unseen Will.

'But you're not pure, are you?' shouted Hyper in a shrill shriek.

Will's blood boiled. He made a fist around the scar on his palm. 'No, I'm not now, but you forget one thing. I have been tainted by your mistress,' he said whilst glaring at them.

'How does that make any difference?' Hyper said, as he jostled on Endo's back for a better hold.

'It makes all the difference. Being tainted will disguise my true purpose. Now shut up and just follow in silence! I can't reveal our true intent until we've broken through the seal,' Will said.

'And how do we do that?' Endo exclaimed.

'You'll see, but first we need Lysis to show up,' Will huffed.

'Why?' Hyper asked.

'Because he is the Gatekeeper to the Oasis and he is going to let you in unawares. Like you said, I can't freely come and go now because I'm impure. So on those occasions, Lysis is obliged to vet me for entrance. But by merely his presence alone, the reveal of the Oasis will show you the way. Then you can seize your chance, impure or not.'

'Will you not be joining us?' Endo said, concerned.

'No. If we are spotted together, then Lysis will sense a trap and it will all be over.'

'I thought you'd never met Lysis?' Endo said gruffly.

'No, we haven't, but I know protocol for these circumstances and that means the Gatekeeper must show up to authorise approval for a tainted wishing to seek solace with Thalamus. Now, again! Quiet! Let me do my thing and you will know when the time is right,' Will said, feeling flustered at the apparent lack of understanding of the foul pair. Letting the message sink in, Endo and Hyper did as requested.

Eventually Will fell silent from whistling and in hushed tones, added, 'I've now reached the wall that surrounds the Oasis. I cannot go any further. Endo, Hyper, I need you to take cover in the trees and wait for Lysis to show.'

Endo did as Will asked and made for the wooded

area. He still couldn't fathom out why he couldn't see the path of flowers or the wall that allegedly protected the Oasis. He hoped he wasn't being led up the garden path. He pulled Hyper from his back and plonked him on a nearby branch.

*

Will sat on the crumbling wall and eyed the skies. He hoped Stan would succeed in taking down Thrombus, but not triumph in returning to his life. Will was damned if he was to be left here to rot in limbo for all eternity with no reward, while Stan got another shot.

Will vowed that if he had been given a second chance at life all those years ago, then he would have saved himself instead.

As he sat there in his dark mood he glanced over to Endo, who was standing with his arms crossed in a recess of a tree, and above him on an overhanging branch stood Hyper, who was holding on to the tree for support, surveying the skies.

Will knew he couldn't let them stick around once he had the winged key, but for now they were the best he had to overthrow Lysis. Once he had the key and Thalamus was destroyed, the sacrifice for revealing the Oasis to Endo and Hyper was worth the admission. Just so long as Venous had the winged key and not the Heparin, all would be fine.

Will didn't want Stan to fail in eradicating Thrombus. He wouldn't wish brain death on him, but he could live with himself if Stan awoke in a vegetative state. At least Stan would get a taste of what it was like to live in limbo.

*

Lysis came flitting down and followed the path of wild flowers, almost brushing them with his abdomen, sending pollen and petals to the four corners of the wind.

He caught sight of Will sitting on the wall and slowed his approach. He felt danger all around, but couldn't place it.

'I presume you are the Will that Stan speaks of?' Lysis said as he came to rest before the border.

'William Last. Yes. And you are Lysis?' Will enquired as he pushed off the wall to greet him.

'I am. Now why am I here? I felt you make contact with the seal but not pass through. Why is that?'

'The opening to the Oasis. Yes. I'm afraid I've been tainted and cannot now pass,' Will said, showing Lysis his semi-healed palm.

'That should not prevent you passing through,' Lysis said, feeling anxious and vulnerable. 'It only works on the impure of this world,' he said. 'Are you impure?'

'As Stan's Guardian, I can assure you I have no impure qualities in me. I am as troubled by this as you. What should I do? I really must speak to Thalamus as a matter of urgency.'

'I cannot let you pass through, Will. There is too much at stake. I know the Virchow's Triad seek the Oasis to taint. I must stop them before that happens. My presence here is enough to reveal the location to them, as I share a bond with the seal,' Lysis said in dismay.

Will circled Lysis and watched him turn to face him. 'Then let me help you. if I trust you with what I need to speak to Thalamus about, will you trust me to help you?'

Lysis looked deep into Will's eyes. 'Okay, tell me what is so important and if I believe you then maybe we can journey together?' he said, regarding Will cautiously.

'Venous has the key in her possession,' Will said, acting concerned.

'Which key are you referring to?'

Will glanced past Lysis and said, 'A small key in the shape of wings adjoined by a symbol.'

'And what of it?'

'It is the key that will grant her access to the Oasis, to pass through the seal. If she does that, then I don't need to tell you what will happen and there will be no stopping her from tainting the Oasis,' Will lied.

'How did you come by this information?' Lysis quizzed.

'I got the information from a short Triad member. Goes by the name of Hyper. It was he who tainted me with this scar,' Will again lied to further distance the connection between him and Venous.

'This is very troubling, as I haven't long left Stan behind. When did she acquire it?'

'She has been tracking you, is all I know, Lysis. She must have seized an opportunity when you parted ways.'

'...Okay. If what you're saying is true then we must

take it back, regardless of whether Stan succeeds in his mission or not. If we have the key and all else fails, then he still has a small glimmer of hope,' Lysis said. Will nodded in agreement and smiled.

Will approached Lysis and looked to his abdomen. 'You look injured. Will you be fine to take on the Virchows?' he mused.

'For now, yes, but with your help then I think we can destroy them together. Far easier than I can achieve on my own.'

'Good, then let's combine our efforts, Lysis. Let us take down the Virchow's Triad together.'

With that, Will approached Lysis who extended a leg for him to use, and he stepped up to climb onto his back. Then they began to rise. Will glanced over to the empty space where Endo and Hyper had been hiding and knew that they had taken their opportunity to cross through the seal into the Oasis.

All Will cared for now, was ownership of the key and for Thalamus to no longer be a threat, once Endo and Hyper had become the new custodians of the Oasis. Then it would be easy. The Triads could then be slain with the help of Lysis. The winged creature could then be taken care of by Will's own hands and the key in his grasp would unlock his salvation. As for Stan, he would become aimless and lost.

*

Endo couldn't believe his eyes when the veil fell. One moment there were rolling hills, the next a path had appeared from out of nowhere, revealing Lysis and Will engaged in conversation by a derelict wall.

He seized the time and snatched a startled Hyper from above, throwing him over the wall.

Hyper, sensing what was happening, pirouetted in the air and curled into a ball, barrel rolling across the threshold and out of sight.

Endo ducked down behind the tree and waited for the coast to be clear before he attempted a climb over.

No sooner had the conversation came to an end and Endo was happy, the peculiar fly and Will had left them behind. The veil then began to close.

Endo shouted to Hyper in astonishment. 'The wall has vanished from view again and the path is shrinking in form. Toss me the end of your whip quickly, so I can pull myself over.'

Hyper did as requested. But Endo could not see the crumbling façade anymore, just an image in his mind of where it was. Then out of the invisible veil, three spiked talons came from nowhere and buried into the ground beside him.

Grabbing on, Endo made his ascent over. The feeling of climbing into nothingness baffled him, but eventually he was over and through. Hyper stood waiting between two large pillars, beaming like a happy child.

'What now, Endo?' Hyper said, retracting his whip as his companion came into view.

'Now we seize this place for our own. Unsheathe your whip, Hyper, and let's raze this place to the ground. Then we can pull these pillars down and when we've done that, we will turn our attention to the island. The moat is already tainted so we will have no problem there.'

'Can we torch the island too? Can we, Endo?' Hyper said, jumping around with glee.

Endo unfurled his whip and lashed it towards the fauna growing up between the pillars. It entwined around the plethora of vines and hooked in. He focused his dark energy from within, that shot along his arm and up through the whip, to the talons at the end. They erupted into a fiery inferno, catching everything alight that they touched. The fire soon spread out of control.

'Do as you wish, Hyper. Let's turn this place from an Oasis of Hope into a Pit of Despair,' he said with a malicious grin.

Hyper caught the glare from the steel chalice on the island, as he looked around for what to burn first. 'What about that over there?' he said, pointing.

Endo met his gaze. 'We were told by Will not to touch that. Something to do with his salvation... but I say do it. He is not here to get in our way... so I say damn him to hell,' he said malevolently.

Hyper's eyes lit up. To him this was the ultimate way to get revenge on Will for all the hurt he caused him, and if that meant taking away his only salvation then so be it. Hyper suddenly became very happy with himself.

Endo looked on at the ruin he was causing, safe in the knowledge that Thalamus would soon be destroyed, with Thrombus taking hold of all.

For Endo, the picturesque landscape made him sick to his stomach. The sooner they could raze it to the ground, the more agreeably it would sit with him.

16

THROMBUS

Kneeling in the throne room at the top of the tower, Stan looked around nervously. To his right, curled into a ball lay De'Ath. Behind him, stood a triumphant Venous brandishing the winged key.

Stan hadn't had the energy left to put up much of a fight downstairs and so reluctantly had agreed to climb the stairwell, again under duress. De'Ath was thrown over Venous' shoulder and carried up in a weak and fragile state.

On arrival Stan was smashed in the back of his knees by the sharp edge of Venous' kite, forcing him down onto the stone floor, where he had the key seized from his possession.

A lone tilly lamp swung high from a chain above his head, the flame from within lighting up only fragments of the room, causing shadows to dance menacingly across the parquet brick flooring.

Stan looked out to the window cut into the east-facing wall. Paneless and arched, giving him a glimpse of the stormy sky, with flecks of lighting streaking across.

He could just make out in the centre of the room, a tall throne that seemed to glisten red with each passing of the tilly lamp's light.

On further inspection, he could see the backrest was fashioned into two large wings that fanned out like those of a bat in flight. Between the wings' join, jutted the back of a bald, red, skinless head.

A network of veins similar to the vein that held De'Ath captive in the torture chamber downstairs, spread out from the occupant of the throne in a web-like structure. They branched off like shoots, into the walls and ceiling.

The feeling of dread and nausea coursed through Stan and echoes of his past actions flashed in his mind. The loss of Heparin, the failed rescue of De'Ath, and the relinquishing of the winged key, all futile now that he had finally made it to this moment. No hope left to ever see Petra or the girls ever again.

Venous strode past him and knelt before her master, offering up the key. 'Thrombus, I bring you the key that was designed by Thalamus to smite you. I also bring you Stan himself, robbed of hope along with his friend De'Ath, who were both trying to escape when I found them.'

A heavy, laboured breathing came from the throne. 'Do... not offer... me... the key, Venous. It... could still... do me harm.'

'Sorry, ma'am,' Venous said, taken aback. 'I will take it far away, just as soon as you tell me what to do with it,' she added alarmingly.

'I want you to... go meet your brothers... They have taken... the Oasis... Once there... I want you... to bury it somewhere... safe,' came the shallow reply.

'As you wish, mistress. What of the prisoners?' Venous said, casting a sneer to Stan.

'Bring... me... De'Ath.'

Venous rose to her feet and went to collect De'Ath, pulling him up. She then steered him around the throne to face Thrombus.

On seeing Thrombus, De'Ath let out a blood curdling cry that echoed around the walls.

'Bring him... in close... to me,' Thrombus ordered.

Venous did as requested and pushed him face to face with her mistress. De'Ath recoiled in horror and tried to turn his head away. 'Such a... handsome man... Won't you... kiss me?' Thrombus said.

De'Ath tried to fight but he was too weak and Venous too strong.

Thrombus leant forward and in a sickening instant, Stan saw the pair embrace. De'Ath was screaming as their lips entwined. But no sooner had they locked lips, De'Ath began to convulse as Thrombus began to suck the life force from him, draining him and turning him grey.

Stan was in conflict. He wanted to save his friend but it all happened so fast and he was too weak and petrified to help. In the end he sank his head in shame.

De'Ath became just like the lost souls that Stan had encountered earlier, all recognition of his former self waning forever.

Venous then uncoupled the empty husk of De'Ath from her mistress, marched him to the window, smiled to Stan, and threw De'Ath through the arch, to join the throng of fellow lost souls drifting in the moat below.

'I'm sorry, old friend,' Stan said under his breath, as tears formed in his eyes.

Thrombus licked her lips. 'That's... much better... Leave Stan... for me... now, Venous... and be... on your... way.'

'Enjoy your final moments, Stan,' Venous said as she made her way past him to the door and flashed him a snide wink.

Stan watched Venous exit and the door shut behind her, and gulped before turning back to face his fate.

'I've waited... a long time... to meet... you in person... Stan,' Thrombus said as Stan looked back her way.

Stan could not bring himself to answer and just knelt there, all forlorn and ashen.

As Thrombus arose from her throne, Stan noticed that the wings that formed the backrest weren't some decorative addition but in actual fact joined to her spleen. As she rose so the wings retracted, concertinaing in on themselves.

The network of veins that held her steadfast also broke free and began to swish about, sending their dark red fluid dripping to the floor.

Then turning to face Stan, the base of Thrombus' wings brushed against two lifeless grey souls that were on all fours acting as her seat. Knocking them over, she cut them a curt nod and they reassembled their position.

The sight that befell Stan transfixed him in terror. Towering at over eight feet tall, the bloody form that was Thrombus honed into view, dragging her blood-wet wings behind her, streaking the floor.

Stripped of all skin, Stan could see every artery, every muscle and every pumping vein that made up Thrombus' DNA.

She resembled the female form in every way but her belly was bloated and taut. Stan could tell that she had certainly been having her fill, feeding off souls.

The bloated, crimson, sinewy form approached him and her lidless eyes seemed to bore into his very soul as if she was sizing him up for her next snack.

Stan leant back on the balls of his feet as the grotesque form shambled over and cupped his chin in her hand, transferring blood to his face.

A large forked tongue extended from her mouth and snaked around his head. The forked tips seeming to probe his skin and taste his fear.

She studied him for some time, then recoiled her tongue on removing her hand. 'I thought... you would... be more... imaginative... than this,' she said, as she pointed both hands at herself and followed the flow of her twisted body.

'I, I, didn't create you,' Stan stammered.

'No, not what... I am... granted... Stan, but what... you perceive me... to look like,' she said, still eying him coolly. 'Still... it doesn't matter... This form... will suit me... just fine,' she added, between paused breaths.

'So what now? You've got what you want. What happens to me now?' Stan said, although he didn't

114

want to hear the answer.

'I haven't decided... your fate yet... but I do need... to tell you... a story about... how I first... arrived here,' she mused.

'I had an accident that created you. What's there to tell?' Stan said, trembling.

'Yes you did... but not recently... You see, I've been waiting dormant... since forming... from your first... head trauma... when you were six years old... It was only a minor accident... and not one... to give me great hold over you, but the accident you had recently... was the catalyst... for you finally ending up in a coma... and gave me sway... over you now.'

'But, but I was cured as a child,' Stan said, shaking.

'Part cured. I was always there... in your darkest thoughts, held at bay... waiting... Watching... even through the manifestation of your phobia.'

'William Last never told me any of this,' Stan replied, astonished.

'Why would he? William Last... died saving you... when you were six... and he's looked out for you... ever since...'

Stan watched Thrombus walk over to the window and cupped his head in his hands. 'I would have remembered,' he said, trying to take in the revelation.

Thrombus looked out at the white flashes in the dark clouds and said aloud as if in deep thought, 'You had a blunt trauma, you blacked out... and erased the memory from your mind... In its place your hodophobia formed... but now you are conquering... your phobia and being in my presence... will allow me to unlock... that dark secret to you. You see... I am a direct connection... to your Thalamus... and I am going to open up... your locked memory... and reveal... to you... what truly happened.'

She turned from the window and looked at him again; the flashing display lit up her skeletal face. 'William Last... was the... driver of... the oncoming... vehicle that... drove you off... the road.' Her teeth bared bright. 'Six people... died that morning.'

Stan did the maths in his head. It all added up now. Six did perish – four children, the bus driver... and the driver of the other vehicle.

If he hadn't locked himself away for all that time after the tragic event and went to church to pay his respects, then maybe he would have made the connection from the memorial.

'Tell me, Thrombus. What really happened following the crash that morning?' Stan said as he massaged his temples.

Thrombus looked at him with a dark reflection. 'It started out... like any other day...'

17

WILL LAST'S TESTAMENT

Will drove his beat up old banger through the country roads, slicing the bends in order to straighten the road out. The rain began to spatter his dirty windscreen and so he flicked on his wipers. They flicked left and right, smearing the dirt across his vision. He cursed at not getting new wiper blades and proceeded to flick the switch to spray the water jets to the glass, but the bottle was empty. He cursed again.

His CB radio crackled into life and startled him, causing him to veer in towards a row of blackberry bushes that lined the road. He wrestled the steering wheel and pulled sharp to avoid it.

A voice came over the airwaves, Will recognised it as a woman that he had past conversations with. Will enjoyed their talks, it was as if she was the only one who truly understood him.

She never revealed her real name and only stuck to her handle of "Tomb Rush".

She often greeted him with a cheery morning message, but today she seemed off. Will asked if she was fine, but she rebuffed his question and instead asked how his morning was going.

He picked up the receiver and depressed the button. He explained that this morning had started out lousy, with his car failing to start first thing and how he was going to be late for his weekly appointment.

She laughed and told him to lighten up. That no matter how crappy your day was going to be, someone else would always have a worse day.

Will replied that he doubted it. He said that he always got anxious the morning of his appointment.

She then asked him what his weekly meetings were about and Will, without thinking, responded that they were to identify if he actually did have voices in his head telling him what to do.

He cursed again for opening up to a stranger, but for some reason it just seemed right. He couldn't understand it.

Tomb Rush fell silent for a while, before suddenly asking him outright if he had schizophrenia. That stung Will. He was only too well accustomed to the term coined for his condition but it was not something he liked to discuss openly. He tried to change the subject to the weather turning bad, but she wasn't having any of it. The subject soon came full circle back to his condition when she mocked him, saying her voice might actually be in his head too.

Will grew annoyed with her and scolded her for being so insensitive. He lost his temper and told her to mind her own business, almost pulling the mic away from the socket in rage, but she told him to calm down.

As he sped along, the road became slippery. Autumn leaves gathered on the country road, collecting in potholes and spreading out across the tarmac.

Tomb Rush spoke to him again but more gently this time, and asked if this route she had recommended to him weeks ago was far quicker than the one he normally took. Will agreed that it was but added that although it was quicker, there were more hazards along the way. Sharp blind bends and untreated roads just a few of the problems. Not least the high ravine that he travelled on. It overlooked the Mala Sort River to his right that sat nestled below it.

She then said something that struck Will as being odd and out of character. She said that if all went well today then he wouldn't have to worry about his voices telling him what to do anymore. It would become less intrusive.

He pressed her for what on earth she meant by that and her response was that today could be the day that the doctors found a cure. She said Will should be a glass half full kind of man, not half empty.

He took what she said as a backhanded compliment and tried to dismiss the whole conversation, but still the niggling feeling that something was off jarred his mind.

The rain began to fall harder and Will turned his headlights on. He was thankful that something worked as they shone up the dark, narrow road ahead.

Then suddenly, from out of nowhere, Tomb Rush shouted to him to brake hard and without question he did, like a loyal, obedient servant, frozen in fear.

His car locked up and slid out of control on the wet leaves on the road. A hard left bend swung into view and Will yanked hard right on the steering wheel, turning his knuckles white as his car went into a sideways skid.

An oncoming white minibus mounted the bend on the other side of the road and for a brief second both drivers looked at each other in fear. Will slung his steering wheel left to avoid it and the other driver did the same, but Will tailed into the bus, spinning it around so its tail end swung out over the ravine.

Will was thrown back into his seat on impact and his car flipped onto its roof. As he careered off into the undergrowth, from the corner of his eye he saw the bus teetering on the edge before it finally gave way and slid backwards out of sight.

He didn't know how long he hung there, upside down in his car, but his head was throbbing and blood was seeping from his mouth and trickling into his eye.

The female voice crackled into life again and told him to free himself and get down to the river quickly. He had a life to save.

Will didn't bother to press the button on the receiver as he finally understood now that the voice of Tomb Rush was indeed in his head. He cursed her for forcing him to take the actions that he did, but guessed it would have no relevance as it was only his own voice telling him what to do anyway.

He reached for his seatbelt buckle and pushed the release. He fell crumpled onto the roof and in a dazed state pulled himself free from the wreckage.

Will wandered aimlessly to the edge of the ravine and peered over. He saw the minibus on its side, filling up with the fast-flowing rapids.

Looking for a safe passage down, he went into a panic as the minibus began to completely submerge. He decided to slide down as quickly as he could on the slippery slope and as he did so, a child's voice screamed up from below.

Reaching the bus, his left foot got stuck in the mud and as he pulled his foot free, his shoe came away, leaving it wedged behind. He hoisted himself up onto the vehicle's side and saw a frightened child peering back up at him through the smashed window. Sodding wet and freezing, the child's teeth chattered, as he looked to Will, pleading for help.

Will pulled the remnants of the smashed window free and cut his hands to shreds. He began to lose focus, as blood drained from his hands.

He reached in and saw the child was in distress. The child was held fast by his seatbelt. Will, with adrenaline coursing through his veins, searched frantically in his pockets and found his army knife. Without further thought he leant in and hacked at the safety belt, freeing the child.

Tomb Rush's voice laughed manically in his head and told him that he wouldn't save the child. He shouted at her for silence, as he reached in and pulled the child clear. He screamed at Tomb Rush that he had beaten her! He was going to save the boy!

But just as the boy was through the empty window, the minibus slid further into the river, throwing Will off balance. In a final desperate act,

Will threw the boy to safety at the bank's edge, just as the bus began sinking to its doom.

Will, still struggling to stand upright, slipped on the wet metal, his sock having no traction on its surface as he fell backwards with the bus's lurch and in through the open window head first.

Tomb Rush jeered at him that it was him she wanted all along.

The minibus would become his final resting place as he was tangled in with the bodies and seats as it sank into the dark depths.

The boy who had been thrown screaming to the bank had hit his head on a nearby rock. He blacked out instantly, but at least he would survive.

For Will, he sacrificed himself for another, but at least the voice in his head became still as the icy depths took their claim on his soul.

Thrombus finished her story with a wicked grin on her face as Stan became more subdued.

'So that... is the demise... of William Last. His last... will and testament,' she said mockingly.

Stan looked up to her hulking form. 'So you got him killed then? You were the voice of Tomb Rush, the voice in his head that made him do what you wanted.'

'Yes, Stan... I was... and I still am...' she said as she reminisced over her wicked past deeds. 'A man... is so easily... manipulated,' she grinned.

18

THAT OLD GREY MATTER

Venous stood at the inner rim of the moat. The gate had long shut behind her and now she found herself pondering how to get over to the other side of the river.

She thought better of swimming across, as it would be too dangerous for her to even contemplate. The lost souls that inhabited its murky waters could be commanded, but they were unpredictable. One false move and they would turn on her in an instant.

As she waited there, an idea began to form in her mind. If she could command them, then maybe they could carry her across, but she couldn't dare touch the water, for they could mistake her as just some other prey to claim to swell their ever growing ranks.

Deciding to summon them anyway, she beat three times on the surface of her shield. Within seconds the water began to churn, as the lost souls rose to the surface, in a plethora of flailing hands and arms. As the bodies emerged, some were surfacing to the floating debris of the destroyed bridge and quickly pushed the splintered planks away to their neighbour, who in turn did the same.

It was then she knew what to do. She commanded them to mass together to form a line that stretched the width of the river. When that was done she barked at them to huddle together tightly as they bobbed at the surface. She knew it wasn't a big ask, as they still had some form of intelligence and their numbers were plenty.

Once she was happy that they had done as requested, she threw her shield to the moat's edge and strapped her foot through the harness. With her other foot, she kicked off from the ground and jumped into the waiting throng.

It worked like a charm. Hands grabbed the edge of her shield and began to push and pull her along. Any that got out of hand, she lashed with the whip and they peeled away, creating a void to be filled just as quickly by another soul, eager to get to the surface.

Eventually she made it safely to the other side to join the charred landscape that stretched out before her.

It was just in time, too, as in the far-off sky she saw the impending arrival of the winged Lysis, carrying Will upon his back. She readied her stance and brought her shield in close over her arm, her whip unfurling loose by her side.

As Lysis pulled up close to her, Will jumped off his back and aimed for Venous' torso, but she was swift. She dropped to her knees and brought the shield in over her head. Will hit the shield full on and Venous sprang to her feet, knocking him far and wide into the charred ground, sending up black wispy flakes.

Lysis circled around her flank to get her off guard but she pivoted on the spot and let loose her whip. It made contact with Lysis' legs, winding around them, pulling them tight. She then pulled hard and brought him hurtling hard into the ground, covering him in soot. 'Is that all you've got, boys?' she jeered.

Will pulled himself up and approached her cautiously. 'No, Venous, we're just getting started,' he said as he cast off his dusty overcoat.

'Oh really, Will? Then show me what you've got,' she taunted.

Will ran at her and threw his coat at her head, obscuring her vision momentarily, just as she went to knock him back with her shield. He then dived at her legs and took her down, releasing the whip from her grasp.

Lysis pulled his bound feet up to his mouth and cut through the whip with his mouth, severing it cleanly in two.

Will tried to keep Venous pinned down, but she was thrashing about in hysterics. She cast her shield away and head-butted him, sending him backwards. Then she was back on her feet, with rage in her eyes. 'That was a cheap trick, Will. I dare you to try that again!' she yelled.

Lysis seized the opportunity and came flying in at her back. His wings beat down hard on her, pushing her into Will's open arms.

Will forced her around and locked her arms tight as Lysis came in closer and flicked his tail at her sternum. The force sent her and Will both spinning to the moat's edge, sending a cloud of soot to the wind.

A lost grey soul shot out an arm and seized Will's ankle. In a triumphant gurgle it tried to pull him in. Will kicked it away and backed away in alarm.

Venous shot Will a terrible look and backed away from him, keeping a space between her and an approaching Lysis.

'Hand over the key,' Lysis demanded.

'Over my dead soul,' she retorted. Then, 'I command you, free yourselves and join me in the fight,' she said, looking to the moat.

Will wondered what on earth was going on and decided to regroup with Lysis. The pair exchanged a troubled look.

A commotion erupted from the moat, a frenzy of bodies rose out and began to pull themselves onto the charred, barren landscape.

Lysis looked worriedly at Will as hundreds of lost souls began to converge on their position. 'This isn't good, Will,' he said.

Venous backed away from the pair and pointed to the mass of bodies 'That old grey matter is going to end the both of you,' she said with a delicious grin.

Will darted for Venous' shield, snatched it up and backed away towards Lysis. 'Do you think if I climbed on your back and used this shield as a battering ram, that we could push them back?' he said, feeling doubtful.

Lysis eyed the advancing horde and looked to the sneering Venous, who was backing away from the mass of grey bodies. 'We don't really need to attack them head-on. Venous is the only target we need.

Let's say we even the playing field,' he said, as Will made his way over, brandishing the shield.

'I think I know what you have in mind. It's a long shot, but it just might work,' Will said as he clambered on.

Venous thought the pair were fleeing the battlefield and had a momentary lapse in judgment as a nearby wandering soul latched onto her arm. She yanked away in astonishment and forcefully kicked it in its midriff, bowling it into its fellow souls, scattering them like dominoes.

Lysis and Will flew ahead of the mob and swooped round and above the head of Venous, drawing the army around to meet her.

Venous cursed when she realised what they were up to and began to chase after Lysis and Will with the lost souls now at her heels.

'Circle around and fly head-on at Venous,' Will insisted.

'Okay Will, just make sure you don't miss!' Lysis yelled over the roar of the wind.

'I'll guide you once I'm in position. Stay at this height till the last minute and drop to Venous' chest height when I tell you to, and glide towards her when we're close. I'll drop the shield in front of your head and pull it tight. Just let gravity take over, okay?' Will said, feeling nervous.

'Just make sure you remove it before we hit the party,' Lysis said with trepidation.

Will looked across Lysis' beating wings and gave him a weak smile. 'Ready... Wait for it... NOW!'

Lysis descended as Will instructed and Will dropped the shield over his head and used the shield's strapping to rein it in against Lysis' head.

Venous, who was running flat out towards them, kept looking back over her shoulder and was amazed at how quick the lifeless souls were approaching. She turned her gaze around too late just as the shield hit her full on with force and sent her reeling into the frenzied mass.

Will removed the shield and having his vision returned, Lysis pulled sharp to the sky, just as the hands from the throng reached out to grab him. They sailed cleanly overhead.

The army of bodies were on Venous in an instant, clawing her and stripping off her armour as she lashed out and kicked in despair to escape.

Lysis shouted to Will, 'OK, now what? How do we get the key off her?'

'We wait. Look, she is in the middle of the mass, fighting them off. As soon as she has thinned their numbers, we swoop down and pluck her up. She will be so weak that we can just remove the key and drop her off, if you know what I mean?' Will grinned, although he felt pessimistic.

Lysis stopped in mid-air and hovered above the sprawling bodies. 'Just say the word then, and we will do as you request,' Lysis said.

Venous was on her feet and lashing out at the attackers, punching and kicking them off, but with every one she beat back another took its place. She cursed at them and commanded that they let her be, but it was useless, for as soon as Lysis and Will were safely away, the souls had lost all interest in them and came bearing down her, as if they somehow knew that she was the cause of all their pain and were now looking for redemption.

Time passed and eventually Venous gave up the fight and the flock of bodies overwhelmed her. They hoisted her up and began to make their way back to the moat, carrying her above their shoulders.

'What the hell are they doing now?' Will asked, puzzled.

'It would seem they have gotten their quarry and are going to take her with them to their demise,' Lysis said flatly.

'But we must have the key before it is lost forever,' Will said, becoming ever more anxious.

Lysis thought long and hard. 'Right then, Will, I will descend above her just out of reach and you retrieve the key,' he exclaimed.

Realising that they didn't have much time to argue before the swarm hit the moat, Will just nodded and braced himself for the dive.

Swooping down low, Lysis hovered above Venous' sprawled body as she was carried along. Venous caught sight of him and mouthed to him to save her. 'The key first,' Lysis replied in hushed tones, for fear of attracting the attention of the souls who seemed to not be aware of his presence.

Venous knew her time was running out so she reached inside her breast armour and retrieved the key. She held it feebly out for Lysis to get a hold of.

Lysis took hold of it and bent his leg back for Will

to take it off of him. Will stowed it in his coat with glee in his eyes.

'Should we rescue her?' Lysis asked.

Will seemed too distracted to listen to what Lysis was saying, let alone care. He was too lost in thought about the key. 'No, leave her be, it's not our problem anymore.'

'It is my duty to eradicate the Triad, Will, but not like this. Where's your honour in battle?' Lysis said, confused.

'Screw that, it's just one last member for you to worry about. She deserves her fate,' Will said hazily as they hung back from the crowd.

The moat was fast approaching and Venous began to whimper. She did not want to bow out this way. To spend an eternity in a watery grave. A pang of remorse began to eat away inside her as she came ever closer to joining that of her victims' fate.

'No!' Lysis shouted. 'I cannot let it be this way, she must fight me as my equal.'

Will looked solemnly at Lysis. 'Have it your way, but I will have no part in it,' he said as he casually swung his leg over Lysis' body. 'All the best, Lysis, and good luck,' he added as he slid off his back and threw himself to the ground.

Lysis couldn't believe his eyes as Will hopped off but shrugged it off, vowing to save her himself. He sped across the tops of the heads and lowered a foot for Venous to grab on to.

Feeling more hopeful, Venous shot out an arm and grabbed on, hoping to be pulled up and away without alerting her captors, but a deafening whistle pierced the air. Will, getting the attention from the grey matter, pointed at Lysis and shouted, 'Sorry old friend,' before turning and hurrying away.

Lysis reeled in shock and tried to fly away but Venous was holding him tight. The bodies carrying her stopped in their tracks and getting a better hold of her, began to pull her down into a scrum. She screamed in frustration as they tugged her down and she tried desperately to use Lysis to claw her away from their grasp, but it was no use. They were overpowering the both of them.

Will watched on with a sense of relief as Lysis' wings vanished into the mass of bodies signalling the end of him and Venous. He then flicked out the key and studied it in his palm. He smiled at his betrayal. *Just two more to take care of now, then,* he thought, as he made his way to the Oasis.

It was all going to plan, the voice told him, and soon he would take his rightful place in paradise.

19

THE HEPARIN

Stan closed his eyes and tried to remember all the good times that he, Petra, and the girls shared. With each happy thought an even sadder one swam into view. He knew he had been selfish in his attitude of attempting to get better. All the opportunities they could have taken to travel and see the world. Instead they were all passing their time by, being rooted in one place.

He knew the girls would be grown up soon and then they would leave the nest and fly far away to go see the bounties that the world had in store for them. Then it would be just him and Petra all alone.

He sensed that Petra would become restless and that she would probably end up leaving him and so too might just get up and go and pack her bags forever. Leaving him all alone in the world with nowhere to go because he could never unshackle from his phobia, that held him back in all he did.

Maybe it would be best if he did not recover, as that would save them the pain of leaving him. At least this way, they would eventually move on into a brighter world without him, free of his burden upon them.

But no, he didn't want to see himself in that future. It was time to change. To get his life back on track and be in control of his own destiny once more. Life was for living, for seeing and experiencing new things, and who better to share it all with than his family?

He decided there and then that enough was enough. He would lock his phobia away and open the door to new discoveries, to enjoy life to its fullest. But the truth was, he was stuck here now, with no hope of ever getting back home and his one chance had passed him by. He sobbed, as he rocked backwards and forwards, his hands flat on the floor in front of him. A cold, hard reminder of the torment he now faced.

Thrombus interrupted his thoughts. 'As I was saying... Stan, I control Will... by feeding him my voice... Right now, he has taken possession of a key... that he believes will grant him his wings... that Thalamus denied him. A key meant for you, but you see he is wrong... For as soon as he uses it at the fallen Oasis... it will not grant him his desire... not now, the Oasis... is in ruin. It will in fact... allow me to possess him directly... and I will flourish there too, so you see... I will take possession... of your very body and soul.'

Stan heard her words but they sounded like echoes from a far-off place. The image of Petra and his two daughters was at the forefront of his mind.

Then something else, something warm surged through him. A feeling that he could not place. His thoughts ebbed away, as something brushed against his skin. He looked down to his hands and he couldn't believe what he saw. It was Heparin, the kitten he thought he had lost to the souls in the lake.

The fuzzy ball of fur was rubbing against his arms, as it entwined around them and nuzzled its head against him as it completed its circuit. Its purring grew louder as it realised Stan had seen him. Stan brought up his hand to stroke it behind its ears. The purring intensified.

Stan thought he was dreaming and looked around the room to convince himself otherwise. He saw Thrombus still loitering at the window with her back to him and knew that she hadn't seen the kitten. He panicked, not knowing what to do. Afraid that Thrombus would spot the fluffy animal, he went to pick up the kitten but Heparin strode off in her direction.

Stan looked to the kitten through the dimly lit throne room and pleaded for him to come back or hide, but Heparin didn't look back. He casually went up to Thrombus' folded wings and attempted to swipe at them.

Thrombus turned in a rage, thinking it was Stan trying to grovel at her feet to let him go, but as she caught sight of Stan across the room she knew it wasn't so. She threw her big bulk round and saw the kitten staring back at her. He stopped swiping and proceeded to raise his rear leg to lick his fur at the groin.

Thrombus almost shrieked in disgust and her wings shot out into full span. She backed away to the window.

Stan seized the moment and lunged out for the kitten to scoop him up, but Thrombus swung her right wing around and swatted Stan away.

'What... have we... here?' she hollered.

'He's with me, don't hurt him,' Stan blurted out.

'What... is this thing... doing here?' Thrombus demanded, as she snatched up the kitten.

Stan looked affectionately at Heparin. 'it's my fault he is here. I, I killed him and now he is a reminder of my crime,' Stan said, as he extended a hand out to have the kitten returned.

Thrombus dangled the kitten between her thumb and forefinger and held him up to the light at arms' length, observing the kitten, who was trying to swipe at her. She licked her dry cracked lips and spun him around to face Stan.

'I thought... that I was... the monster,' she rasped.

'Please, don't hurt him,' Stan pleaded as tears rolled down his cheeks.

'What... should I do... with him... then, Stanley?' she croaked as the kitten spat and hissed in its suspended state.

Stan wiped the tears from his eyes and bit his bottom lip. He pulled himself to his feet and clenched his fists. 'You're going to let him go or by God I'm going to rip off your wings and tear out your heart... you bitch!' he screamed, feeling the hatred build inside him.

Thrombus just laughed at him. 'You cannot... beat me... you pathetic man,' she said.

Stan rushed at her with his fists flailing, but Thrombus brought her wings round to form a shield. He ran into them, punching at the membrane texture. But with a sudden outward flick of her parting wings she sent Stan backwards, slamming him hard into the wall.

Thrombus extended her drooling forked tongue that then wrapped around the kitten. Releasing him from her hand, she snapped open her mouth and with a slurping sound pulled the coiled kitten into her waiting jaws.

Stan, battered and bruised, looked back in horror as he tried to regain his composure.

Thrombus snapped her mouth closed and swallowed. 'What's... the matter... Stan? Cat... got your tongue?' she said as she patted her belly.

Stan's screams filled the room, as the bloated and contented crimson blob of Thrombus looked on with loathing in her eyes.

20

ASHES TO ASHES

Lysis felt the cool rush of the water rise up to greet him as the grey bodies of souls pulled him under.

Air bubbles escaping from Venous' drowning screams rose up and blurred his vision as he gazed on helplessly in silence. She sunk into the gloom of the murky depths. Her eyes glazing over icy cold as she stared back at him one last time before being claimed by the void.

He thrashed his tail and beat his wings ferociously as he tried to clear himself from the menagerie, but more souls were bearing down upon him and driving him down further.

Lysis began to think it was all in vain, when suddenly a large, grey, male soul, came roaring up through the mass, swatting aside any of its kin that got in its way. The lone soul forced itself up into Lysis' abdomen and started propelling him to the surface. All the other souls that bore down on Lysis fell away as they struggled to maintain a hold, bewildered by the power of this solitary soul.

Lysis broke the surface and immediately flapped

his wings, sending a fountain of water skywards as he twirled up into the dank air.

The single lost soul that saved him bobbed above the waterline and cast a look to the arched window of the tower above. Lysis looked upon him in wonder and then followed his line of sight, puzzled as to what it meant.

It was then that he heard the most deafening, ear-piercing screams reverberate from behind the window, that blocked out even the thunderous sky.

He looked back down to the moat, but the surface was calm again and his rescuer had vanished from view. Lysis hovered there wondering what to do next, and more importantly why he had been saved, but curiosity crept in and he knew that he had to check out the origin of the murderous screams.

He flexed his tail and cast his wings down, then he was off, soaring up the side of the stone tower to see what the commotion was all about.

*

Stan could not believe the sheer tenacity of Thrombus' will to consume Heparin. It all happened so fast and it was so abhorrent to him that her heinous act made him nauseous.

He cried in anguish of having Heparin back one minute only to have him taken away the next. He sat there against the wall, dumbfounded and shocked to the core and all he could think was, *Why?*

Thrombus came shambling over to him and Stan thought that this was the end. He felt he couldn't take any more, but then something unexpected happened.

She began to cough and splutter. Her eyes began to bulge in their sockets and she grabbed her throat as if something had caught in it.

She looked at him in alarm as her tongue rolled out and flapped sickeningly wet onto her bloated stomach. She fell with a crash to her knees and grabbed on to one of the loose veins that swung from the ceiling to steady her large clotted frame.

Stan couldn't understand the spectacle that played out before him and just looked on, perplexed and transfixed by the vulgar sight.

Thrombus tried to speak but she was met with gurgled noises as blood gushed forth from her lips, spraying the room in a crescendo of crimson blood.

Then she arched her back and emitted the most ear-splitting scream that Stan had ever heard.

He noticed a dim light was forming from within her gut and it began to grow with intensity, becoming a brilliant white ball of light that he had to shield his eyes from.

Then she exploded in a fantastic fashion, in a showering array of white burning light mixed with sinew, blood, bone, organs, and muscles.

The whole tower violently shook and trembled. Mortar and brickwork began to fall from the ceiling, freeing the veins that slithered out and fell squirming to the flagstones. Stan tried to get to his feet but slipped on the remnants of Thrombus' blood and guts. Then the tower buckled and started to shift sideways, sending more brickwork crashing down around Stan, as he struggled to unpin himself from hugging the wall.

It then dawned on him, when he was in the dark waters of the moat, a similar white orb of light had guided him to the surface and away from the souls. It had to have been Heparin. Somehow the kitten had radiated the light from within himself and it was enough to deter his attackers.

Now he knew why, it was the same force within Heparin that destroyed Thrombus too when she devoured him. Heparin knew what he was doing all along. He was the anticoagulant that would destroy the haemorrhage from within. His sacrifice was for the greater good. His purpose was accomplished, as was his true intent all along.

The tower began to crumble all around him and Stan felt it start to shift. He pushed himself up and looked to the door behind him. He sensed it would be the wrong move though, as he didn't want the whole place raining down on him and becoming his tomb.

He looked to the window and realised it was his only escape route, but he would have to move fast as the tower began to sink beneath him.

He slipped and slid all the way to the arch and grabbed on to the edge of the window for support. He looked out and saw the moat waiting far, far below. The prospect of meeting the grey souls again didn't fill him with confidence, but he weighed it was better than that of an uncertain fate if he stayed where he was.

He pulled himself up onto the ledge and readied himself for the long plunge.

*

Lysis flew up higher and higher, corkscrewing the conical tower as he made his ascent. When suddenly a large explosion erupted and a searing white light shone out from the tower's window along with thick, glistening, red giblets.

Lysis flung his tail forward and brought his wings back to halt his climb.

The tower then began to rumble, loosening bricks that fell away from the ramparts to descend and splash into the moat below. A large crack appeared from the tower's base and snaked up and around the tower, almost severing it in two. Lysis looked on, bewildered, as it then gave in on itself and sent the tower into a precarious lean.

A dislodged collection of bricks fell away overhead and fell towards him. He beat his wings back in time, narrowly avoiding its path.

The water below began to bubble as froth started to form on the surface, as debris fell into it, heralding a soon-to-be collapse of the entire structure.

The river that flowed in from the west to the moat began to take on a new form as a waterfall, as the moat began to drain away. It seemed to be mirroring on the east-facing too, to the river that flowed away.

Lysis beat his wings and took off again. Driven by an unforeseen urgency to get to the window, it was not unfounded, as no sooner than he pulled up alongside the archway, a familiar character leaped from within.

It took Lysis by surprise as Stan jumped right out in front of him and fell away towards the moat below.

Taken aback by Stan's sudden appearance, Lysis momentarily froze, as his brain processed what was happening.

He stopped beating his wings and fell into a freefall, falling as hard and as fast as a stone.

Lysis hit the water just as Stan was resurfacing, and reached out and grabbed him, just as the ever familiar throng of souls rose behind him to the surface.

Stan was smiling at his good fortune as Lysis whisked him away from harm.

The pair hovered there for a while, congratulating each other and catching up on past events when the tower decided to implode in on itself, sucking itself and the moat down into a massive great newly formed sinkhole.

Stan held on to his friend and looked on in awe as the changing landscape unfolded. 'We have to go and catch up with Will at the Oasis,' he said. 'He has the key that will bring Thrombus back if we don't hurry.'

Lysis shot him a nervous look and without question flew off towards the horizon.

21

DUST TO DUST

The sad, charred form that was Hyper, sat crouched on the top of the last pillar that needed to come down. He was banging his fists down upon its marbled surface in a fit of rage above the lingering smoke that hovered over what was once the Oasis, that had now become a dusty landscape.

Moments ago he had tried to cross the moat to get to the shiny chalice, but no sooner had he attempted to wade in, the water began to churn clockwise at a phenomenal speed.

He was sloshed around the moat and had tried desperately to stay afloat, but the malevolent nature of the water kept pulling him under and spinning him around with increasing intensity.

Endo had approached the fast-flowing water and cast his whip into its depths for Hyper to grab hold of, but Hyper missed it on every turn.

Then to make matters worse, the water had begun to boil, causing steam to form on its surface. Hyper began to scream in agony as the rising temperature of the water began to scald him, stripping the charred skin from his body.

Endo retracted his whip and cast again. This time the talons embedded into the island and Endo pulled tight at his end, creating a firm line. Hyper whipped round and took hold of the line on his next passing and proceeded to pull himself along, back to his waiting companion.

He pulled himself out, shrieking in pain, and made for the remaining pillar, which he threw his whip around and used to climb its surface. There, he sat nursing his wounds until the frustration of not making it across took hold.

Endo sat down, resting on a previously felled pillar and looked up to his troubled brother whilst he recoiled his whip. 'Come down this instance, Hyper! You have brooded long enough. We will find another way to cross,' he said.

Hyper stopped what he was doing and shot Endo a disgruntled look. 'I want that chalice,' he demanded.

'If you come down, then maybe we can use the pillar you're on to form a bridge over it, if we pull it down right,' Endo said weighing up the position of the pillar and the moat.

This seemed to please Hyper and a painful smile spread across his face. 'Yes, yes. That will work,' he said, feeling optimistic.

Endo stood up and outstretched his arms. Hyper jumped from the pillar into his partner's open arms, almost sending Endo back into the moat himself as he made contact.

Hyper uncoupled from his arms and then retreated

to the rear of the pillar and readied himself to topple it over toward the island, as Endo fed his whip around it to take up the slack to pull it toward him.

This was how Will found them when he entered the smoky domain. The pillar had begun to crack and give, as Hyper pushed and Endo pulled, ready to move out of the way when it finally broke free.

With a splintering crack the pillar began to fall forward. Endo turned to move, but Will had sneaked up behind him and using his newly required shield, thrust it forcefully into Endo, pushing him into its path.

Endo stole a look of surprise and anguish at Will as the pillar toppled on top of him. He tried with all his might to stop it crushing him but the weight was too great.

The pillar kept on sliding forward and Endo turned to try and escape but it toppled onto his back, ending his very existence, as the top reached out and crashed onto the moat beyond.

Will turned his attention to the makeshift bridge and spotted the chalice lying on its side next to the granite rock, at the heart of the island beyond. He went to cross the pillar, when a livid Hyper sprang out from behind him and jumped onto his back, sending him flying onto the surface of the white marble bridge.

Hyper rained down hammering blows onto Will's back and screamed in bloodlust as he meant to end Will for killing his brother. The makeshift bridge weakened with each blow, as it struggled to maintain both their weights and began to splinter.

But Will was quick to recover and flipped onto his back. Again he thrust the shield forward, but this time at Hyper, who was struck hard and fell away to the ashen bank.

Will steadied himself with a newfound purpose and darted across the bridge, turning to see what had become of Hyper, once he made it across safely.

Hyper had recovered and had taken a step onto the pillar, but he looked at the water below with unease.

'Come on then, Hyper. Cross if you dare!' Will taunted as he brought the shield up to protect his chest.

Hyper stepped out onto the bridge and carefully began to make his way across, but the cracks started to appear, web-like at its centre.

Will, seeing the fragile state of the bridge forming, raised his shield and slung it at its midsection.

The heavy shield clanged off its smooth surface and spiralled into the water below, sinking from view.

Hyper laughed manically, thinking that Will's efforts had been wasted, but then the splintering gave way and the bridge caved in, sending both pieces of pillar in after the shield, along with the remains of Endo.

Hyper jumped back at the last minute and barely made it to the start of the moat's outer edge. He cursed after Will at the divide that now separated them.

'It's over, Hyper,' Will sneered, as he turned his back on him. 'I will finally claim my wings and I will be rid of this place... and you forever,' he added with giddy delight.

Hyper paced up and down and looked on with loathing as Will reached down and snatched up the silver chalice. A murderous rage engulfed Hyper as his chances of destroying it and ending Will's quest subsided.

Will held the chalice aloft and brought the winged key from out of his pocket. 'You know, I have this voice in my head that tells me what to do sometimes,' he said whilst admiring the chalice's beauty.

'What does it tell you?' Hyper spat in disgust.

'It tells me that this was going to happen all along. That I would always get my wings, but since I arrived here just now, the voice inside has stopped. I just can't fathom out what that means, can you?' he said, taunting Hyper.

Hyper stared back at him with a haunting expression. 'I hope you rot in hell,' he said flatly.

Will laughed at him. 'So long, Hyper. You will join hell well before I do,' he mocked.

With that, Will laid the chalice flat in the palm of his hand and placed the key within its engraving.

The white of the ethereal key began to burn bright as it started to fuse with the chalice. Will became elated at the thought of his bright prospects. He took the chalice by both handles and held it out in wonder in front of him.

But then the symbol that joined the two wings of the key spun round and faced downwards, and the white glow began to turn a molten red.

Will looked on, horrified, as the chalice then caught alight from the key and began to melt away, creating a silver searing hot liquid that started to run from the handles and down his arms.

Will went to drop the chalice in fright but his hands became fused to the handles. He shook the chalice violently, but he could not cast it away.

He screamed in agony, as the molten liquid began to turn a fiery red and spread across him, setting him ablaze in the process.

Hyper started to jump for joy on the spot at the monstrosity on the island before him. His eyes lit up as Will became engulfed. 'Now you know how it feels,' he laughed fervently.

Will, sensing he had little other choice, ran for the moat and dived in, sending up hisses of steam.

Hyper watched him disappear, as he was carried off by the current and dragged below the surface. He approached the moat's edge and peered in with astonishment.

The water began to slow its pace as Hyper watched in fascination, but then a hot geyser shot out from the surface and sprayed him. He teetered back, suddenly becoming afraid as more geysers formed and billowed into the sky, shooting up like fountains.

That was when he then saw a large pair of wings rising out from the surface. He realised at that point what had happened. These weren't wings that belonged to the pure, these were the wings that belonged to his master.

A large, cumbersome, blood-red form emerged from the river and pulled itself over the lip to the island and crawled off to the centre, where it sat down.

It tried to stand but it was too weak. The turmoil it had endured had taken its toll. Blisters and welts popped and sizzled in patches on its body and it winced in pain.

'Thrombus!' Hyper shouted, as the bloated red form stretched out its wings.

'Yes Hyper, it is me and I am here. I am reborn anew,' she said with her eyes downcast to her fragile form.

'What happened to that traitorous Will?' Hyper said, still looking around the moat.

'He has transformed into me and in good time too. It would seem that he got his wings after all,' Thrombus said as she flexed the wings on her back.

'But what does it mean?' Hyper said jubilantly.

'It means Will is no more and you and I now have a chance to rebuild, but we have one more fight ahead first, before we can truly claim what is ours.'

22

THE PLASMINOGEN EFFECT

The landscape they were leaving behind began to terraform. The dark storm began to move on and the sun was trying desperately to break through.

The vegetation began to sprout up through the cracks in the charred ground and all around pockets of life began to return.

Stan looked down in wonder, but he still felt troubled. If Thrombus was destroyed then he should be cured, the changing vista was paramount to that. But what was green and vibrant that lay ahead was withering and dying now. It was like the evil had shifted elsewhere and had not fully been extinguished, with the storm swinging around to meet them again.

Lysis, sensing Stan's thoughts, said, 'I fear we will not like what we find up ahead at the Oasis, Stan.'

'I think it means Will has used the key and if that is so then I have no way of getting back home,' Stan said, defeated.

'As long as you have me, Stan, then there will always be hope.'

Stan looked to Lysis with admiration. 'Thank you,

Lysis. If what you say is true, then when this is all over, I will never forget you as a friend.'

'When this nightmare ends, you won't remember a thing, but thanks for the sentiment anyway,' he replied. Then, 'Hold on, Stan. We are almost there, are you ready for this?'

For once, Stan was. He had done the impossible and overcome his phobia by journeying to hell and back. Now he was all but ready to go home.

Lysis bore down and swept across the tips of the burnt and twisted trees. His wings thrummed rapidly as he levelled out. 'There is something I think you should know, Stan,' he said.

'Like who is going to fight who, you mean?' Stan said as he pointed dismally below to the two figures. 'If you don't mind, I think I'd like to take Hyper. Can I leave you to deal with Thrombus?'

'That's not what I meant,' Lysis said, feeling a pang of guilt. He decided to leave it for now. 'Very well, let's end this now! After you,' he said, as he swooped down and in for the kill.

Stan slid off Lysis' back and landed at the feet of Hyper. They locked eyes and began to circle one another.

Lysis swooped down to the island and collided with Thrombus. The pair went rolling off into a burning bush, as they wrestled for dominance.

Hyper made his move and lunged for Stan, but Stan grabbed hold of him with both arms and fell backwards to the dirt. Using Hyper's forward momentum to kick him off, he thrust him overhead.

Hyper went sailing into a downed pillar. His blackened chest plate of armour cracked and splintered on impact, exposing the damaged flesh beneath, and his shield was thrown from his back.

Stan raced over and tried to pin him down, but Hyper flipped round and pulled his whip free. He flung it around Stan's waist and pulled him in close, head-butting him.

Stan staggered back, dazed and confused, giving Hyper an advantage to get back on his feet. He circled him and jumped on his back, hooking the whip around Stan's neck, pulling it tightly to try and garrotte him.

Stan fell to his knees with the wriggling Hyper attached and fell forward to try and eject him off, to loosen the whip as it cut into him.

But Hyper would not let go. No sooner had he gone over Stan's head, he twisted around so they were both facing one another. In a last ditch attempt, Stan threw his arms around Hyper in a bear hug, picked him up and ran towards the moat.

Hyper screamed at him to stop, as he was carried onwards. He cast his head to the moat and then back to Stan in terror as they both ran headlong into the boiling hot river.

Lysis rolled away from Thrombus and planted all four feet in the ground. He waited for her to approach and bent his head down low. He arched his back, bringing his three-pronged tail up over his head. The sharp points impaled Thrombus' stomach and pinned her to the ground. Lysis then flicked his tail back and forth, smashing her repeatedly into the soil of the island.

She screamed in between each sickening squelch, as she was pulverised to a pulp.

At last he released her and made his way to the middle of the island, thinking he had left her for dead.

He began to burrow down into the soil and used his wings to disperse the loose dirt as a tunnel took shape. But he left himself exposed and an injured Thrombus crept up behind him.

She shambled over to the pit he was creating and fell onto him with all her weight. Lysis struggled to free himself as her large mass bore down. He had barely the time to register what was happening, when she grabbed hold of his wings and tore them from his back in rage.

Meanwhile, Stan and Hyper were clawing at each other below the surface of the river. Stan was frantically trying to pry the whip away from his neck, but Hyper would not let go.

The water wasn't as hot as Stan imagined, but he could not take it anymore. He kicked for the surface and brought Hyper up with him.

Then, taking a chance, Stan pushed himself toward the bank using the speed of the water and slammed Hyper into the side. Hyper's grip loosened on the whip and it gave Stan a small slither of hope, as he slid out from under it.

He grabbed hold of the whip's three talons that uncoiled below the surface and thrust them up into Hyper's exposed body. Then he turned and kicked himself away, pulling the talons free.

Hyper's shocked expression fell, as blood trickled from his mouth. With a final gurgled word that Stan could not make out, he drifted off with the current, releasing the whip's handle.

Stan fed the whip through his palms, as he buffeted off the far walls of the bank. He felt himself become dizzy as he was spun around the moat. He aimed the whip at the island and lashed it out. The spikes bit in and the whip became taut. He grabbed the handles with both hands, as the current slammed him hard against it. He almost let go as the wind was knocked from him, but his steely determination did not waver as the water tried to choke him down.

With extraordinary effort, he pulled his way along the whip and prayed it would hold as he reached for the edge of the bank.

Thrombus used her legs to pin Lysis' tail down to stop him from trying to spear her again, and forced him round to face her. His large, bulbous eyes gave her a blank stare that she could not read. She felt her life force drain away with her blood that soaked into the freshly dug tunnel. She beat down upon his face and clawed out one of his eyes, leaving its socket exposed in a defiant attempt to end him first.

Just as she was about to tear out his other eye, a sharp pain soared through her back and she was yanked away, cursing and wailing, from him.

Thrombus screamed and thrashed as the realisation dawned on her that Stan was the one who stood towering above her, peering down into the hole, and he had been the one who dealt her the final blow, pulling her off Lysis by the tether of the whip.

She spat a curse at him and pulled the spikes from her stomach, releasing a shower of arterial blood that sprayed over him.

Then Lysis was upon her. He opened his mouth and gorged at her open wounds, drinking in the taste of victory, as her life force drained away.

Stan thought he would find the act distasteful but he was used to seeing worse by now.

'It's over then,' he finally said, as he swung his legs over the hole and sat down on the edge.

Lysis stopped slurping and cocked his last remaining eye at Stan. 'Not quite, I'm afraid, Stan. There is something I need you to know and I have a request I need you to follow.'

Stan slid down the hole and came to rest at Lysis' side. 'Sure, whatever you need, old friend, but tell me first how to patch you up.'

Lysis slumped onto Thrombus' decaying carcass and rolled over to face Stan. 'The Oasis of Hope has faded from here, Stan. Now it will become a memorial to be locked away deep inside your mind of your time spent here. When you awake, you will have no recollection of this ever taking place.'

Stan reached out and placed a hand on his friend. 'I don't understand what you're saying,' he said.

'It means that this part of your brain will never recover. The damage was inflicted many years ago when you were just a child. The Heparin was used on your recent haemorrhage.'

'So does that mean something will be wrong with me when I wake, then?'

'No, it just means that there will be a problem with short-term memory loss, is all, and this journey you have taken will be forever erased from your mind.'

Stan studied Lysis sombrely. 'OK, I get it, that's fine, but what of my memories of you?'

'You will always have my stories in your comics from your childhood, Stan. As for me, I must stay here and feast on this mild clotting until the day you die,' he said, grabbing hold of Stan's hand.

'Right, I think I get it, Lysis, but how will I return home? I mean – wake up from this?'

'You must first bury me alive, here and now,' Lysis said, letting the words sink in.

'But I don't want to kill you,' Stan said, looking at him pleadingly.

'Oh Stan, you won't. I am a Coffin Fly and that is my purpose. I thrive on the dead decaying corpses that are buried, I will never die.'

Stan sat down in the earth and leaned against the tunnel wall, trying to digest the information. 'But how does that help me return to Petra and the girls?'

'When you have covered me over and made your peace, then you will know, Stan. I promise,' Lysis said as he looked out from the hole, to the sun returning overhead.

Stan began to cry at the prospect of abandoning his friend under these circumstances. 'But you don't belong here, Lysis, it doesn't feel right,' he said, wiping his eyes.

'But I am where I belong, Stan. You see, I am your thoughts in all matters. I process the information and send it on.'

'So, what are you trying to say?' Stan said, confused.

'I'm trying to tell you that... I am the Thalamus within your brain and I am exactly where I need to be.'

A smile spread across Stan's face as he finally realised that everything would turn out fine.

'There is just one more thing, Stan, I need to say before we part ways.'

Stan eyed him fondly. 'Yes, Lysis.'

'You take journeys in your mind every day to escape reality and dream of better places, when you are at your lowest. Your mind is a treasured thing of beauty, it finds fair and rational ways to help you overcome obstacles and helps you make sense of it all. But the greatest key, is understanding what you want out of life and to strive for your dreams. Don't let anything pass you by or hold you back, especially that of a phobia.'

Stan sat there a while longer and thought of his happier times before he decided to climb out from the hole.

Lysis said farewell and then carried on burrowing down further, pulling Thrombus down with him. Eventually they disappeared from view and Stan began to fill the hole in.

When all was done, Stan sat on the mound he created and watched the drifting sun pass to the horizon.

The river began to rise up and formed a large body of water that circled him on the desolate island. Then as quick as the wall came into being, it collapsed. It washed over him and chased him and the island, plunging him into a black void.

23

BACK FROM THE BRINK

Petra Palmer paced up and down outside the hospital wing and drew a puff on her cigarette. She was feeling more anxious with every passing day that Stan remained in his coma.

She knew the risks more than anyone else. That if her husband did recover, then he might not return to her as he had once been.

Extinguishing her smoke, she threw it to the floor in frustration and twisted it under her heel. She decided to go and get a coffee from the vending machine inside.

Passing through the clinical passageway, she pulled out her purse and pushed the change around inside, hoping that she had enough on her to put in the machine.

Having the right change, she dispensed herself a cup and inserted in her money.

She leaned up against the wall and blew on the hot beverage as she looked around the waiting room at the sick and infirm who had arrived or had been brought in.

Her mobile rang and it startled her. She spilled her coffee and it splashed onto her arm, scalding her in the process. A nurse nearby looked at her frostily and pointed to a sign on the wall about not having your phone turned on whilst in the hospital.

Petra nodded at her and rolled her eyes at a patient beside as she threw her half-filled cup into the bin and strode back outside.

Swiping the phone, she pulled it to her ear and talked into the hidden mic. 'Hi, Petra speaking. Can I help you?'

A familiar voice answered. 'Hi Petra. It's Natasha from the travel shop.' She waited for a reply.

'Hi. Sorry Natasha, I wasn't expecting your call. It's just been manic here with... you know,' Petra said as she looked to the ground.

'Sure, sure, I understand. If you want me to ring back at a better time I can...'

Petra cut her short. 'No, it's fine. What can I do for you?'

'Well I was just checking in on you really, and hoping to find out if there has been any developments, you know?'

Petra pushed her hair over her ear. 'No, nothing has changed at the moment,' she said as she scuffed her shoes on the pavement.

'Oh, okay. Well, no news is good news, right?' Natasha said, trying to sound reassuring and optimistic.

'I suppose. Look, I should thank you for looking after the girls and I'm really glad you stopped by the other day with those bags of essentials I needed.'

'Nonsense. What are friends for, right? I know it must be tough on you right now, but stay strong, okay?'

'Yeah, sure. Thanks again, Natasha. Look, I should go. I don't like being gone from his side too long,' Petra said.

'That's fine, but if you need anything just ask, okay?'

'I will, and thanks. My parents have the girls now, so they should be fine, but how's my other little soldier doing?'

'Oh, just fine. Always getting into mischief, but hey.'

'Like that, is it? Well if he gets too much then I can contact my folks and make arrangements.'

'Not at all. It's nothing I can't deal with, and besides, I like the company anyway.'

'OK then Natasha, as long as you're cool.'

'Absolutely. Now I'll get off and you go give my love to Stan, won't you?'

'I will, see you later.'

With that, Petra ended the call and switched her phone to vibrate and slipped it back in her pocket before she headed back off to the ward.

By the time she made it back, a nurse was scurrying out of the room with her head down and ran headlong into her.

'I'm sorry,' the nurse said, as she lifted her head to see Petra. 'Oh, Mrs Palmer, it's you. Fantastic news! Your husband's awake.'

Petra almost couldn't believe what the nurse had said. 'I'm sorry, what did you say?'

'Your husband... he just woke up.'

Petra barged past her and butterflies fluttered in her chest, as she darted for his bed. She raced in and there was Stan, sitting up and looking around. The joy she felt was overwhelming.

'Hi baby, the nurses tell me I've been in a coma. Sure feels like it. I had a look in the mirror a while ago and it looks like I've been to hell and back!'

Petra rushed into his arms, crying and laughing at the same time. She hugged him tight and kissed his face, with wet tears rolling from hers. 'Don't you ever leave me again, Stan Palmer. You promise?' she said.

'Alright Petra, alright... Just how long was I out for? It feels like forever.'

Petra just pulled him in tighter and smothered him in kisses.

24

POSTCARD FROM HEAVEN

Natasha turned the travel agent's open sign to closed and locked the door behind her.

She adjusted her handbag on her shoulder and swung it around her waist. She snapped it open and popped the daily post inside then snapped it shut. Turning back, she pushed the button and waited for the alarm to set. She creased down her skirt and looked to her reflection in the window, smoothing her hand through her hair. Satisfied that she looked presentable, she turned and strode off away from town to the Mala Sort River.

Walking past the church, her high-heeled shoes click-clacked along the pavement and echoed across the cemetery.

The summer evening was still and there was no hint of a breeze. She undid the top button on her blouse and pulled a mini fan from her pocket, blowing it across her neck.

The vicar caught sight of her and his face turned red. He wished her a pleasant evening and hurried back off inside.

She carried on her way and made the descent down the hill. She couldn't believe a year had passed already since the day of the freak accident that had almost killed her co-worker.

Having crossed the junction at the foot of the hill, she navigated her way through the turnstile and headed off for the bench. She turned the fan off and returned it to her pocket, switching it for a tissue that she then used to wipe the mildew off the seat.

Natasha sat there and admired the calm and serene view across the river. She often came here after work just to unwind before she headed off home.

She popped her handbag beside her and opened it up. She pulled out a bag of crusts that remained from her afternoon lunch and began to pull pieces out that she then tossed into the river. The ducks that had seemed oblivious to her presence before had now started to converge on her position, and started fighting over the doughy treats.

Still smiling at their petty squabbling, Natasha turned her attention to the post in her bag and reached in to retrieve them. She slung some unimportant ones back into her bag as she thumbed through them and settled on one in particular that had caught her eye. The writing on it was instantly recognisable. It belonged to Stanley Palmer.

Stashing the remaining post in her bag, she snapped back to Stan's one in her hand. She used her long index fingernail and cut through the envelope, revealing a letter inside. She pinched hold of it and slid it out, but a concealed postcard slid out from behind it and landed on her lap.

Giving the postcard no heed for now, she unfolded the letter and began to read it.

Dear Natasha,

I hope this letter finds you well and that my temp is not giving you too much grief. Honestly, I think he has a thing for you, it might be worth you trying your luck there.

Anyway I digress, so getting back to the topic I had in mind, I would like to just tell you that we really do appreciate all you have done for us, from looking after the girls when Petra was with me in hospital and for you visiting me on my rehab sessions. Also I can't thank you enough for picking up my share at work whilst I'm on a long break.

I've got to say that my near death experience really was a life changer. It made me realise just how precious life really is and that I should embrace the unknown and not live in fear of it.

Petra has never been happier and the girls are just ecstatic that they have finally come away on holiday with us all as one family.

I suppose it goes to show that something wonderful can come out of something so terrible and it makes me feel truly blessed. Sure, I still have my off days, but that is to be expected. I do get forgetful from time to time but Petra says she likes the new me, though I secretly think it's because my phobia is well and truly laid to rest.

Talking of rest, I should say that is exactly what I'm doing now. I can't believe I've travelled half the world to experience this, but what an experience it is! Here I am sitting on a bench in the Kawachi Fuji gardens, admiring the flowering Wisteria blooms that are high above my head, creating this wonderful

165

tunnel and taking in the scented fragrance whilst I sit here writing to you.

I know. You're jealous, right? Anyway our whistle stop tour is a long way from its end yet and I have an urge to go soak up the sun and have some "Sake" so I'll wind this letter down.

My biggest reason for writing to you though, is to express my deepest gratitude to you for looking after Heparin while we are away.

I was so distraught and upset at my actions back then, I guess my Karma for chucking him in the river came full circle and that was why I was hit by the coffin.

What were the chances of you making your regular visit to the bench and finding the carrier with him still alive snagged on those bull reeds? I suppose it's true what they say... cats really do have nine lives!

I know my choice of name for him might sound a little unusual, but it was the Heparin that destroyed my clot and saved my life when they administered it into me. The fact that he too survived his ordeal makes me think it was very apt.

Okay, I'm going to close this down now and would like to finish by saying that I will see you on our return and we can catch up over a cuppa.

Hope you enjoy the postcard I sent you. I noticed that you don't have any, so I am extremely happy that mine is the first of hopefully many more that you can have to start your own collection.

Yours thankfully

Stan.

*

Natasha stowed the letter away in her bag and picked up the postcard to examine it. It showed the Wisteria tunnel that Stan had mentioned on its glossy print and had emblazoned across it "A Slice of Heaven". She flipped it over and read the back, it merely said:

Emerging through the tunnel of light to the

hope of new beginnings.

Stan

Natasha smiled to herself and popped it in her bag. She rose to her feet and began to take a long walk home. Back to Heparin, the kitten with nine lives.

25

THE OASIS OF HOPE

The Oasis began to flourish once again, but it was more vibrant and more spectacularly tranquil than it had been before.

A large circular hole in the ground, the Oasis was blossoming. Two waterfalls on opposite sides cascaded down into it and crashed over rocks below, that collected in its vast pool.

Trees sprang up all around above ground and down in the hole, rising from the edges of the cavern, and wildlife had moved in everywhere. The rocky edifice of the hole was moss-strewn and green fauna collected in its nooks and crannies. Ledges jutted out and they contained wild flowers. Butterflies basked on their petals.

The glorious sun beat down and shimmered off the pool's calm surface. Below, koi carp of magnificent colours swam lazily around and some sheltered under large water lilies that floated aimlessly around above them.

Flying insects skimmed the surface and darted to and fro, avoiding the frogs and various amphibians that collected on the lilies.

One particular flying species enjoyed skimming the surface as it thrummed its magnificent wings and danced across the shimmering glow of the pool without fear of predators catching it, it's size too daunting a task for any life that thrived and inhabited there.

The Coffin Fly felt calm and at peace as its shadow blotted out the sun. It made another pass and circled the pool.

Lysis had fully healed and regained all of his limbs, as Stan had over time become ever stronger. Here he was now, as the custodian of the paradise he traversed, restoring harmony in the Oasis of Hope once more.

8130489R00103

Printed in Germany
by Amazon Distribution
GmbH, Leipzig